Copyright © 2023 Shannon O'Connor
All rights reserved.

All rights reserved. No part of this publication may be reproduced, distributed, or transmitted in any form or by any means, except in the case of brief quotations embodied in critical reviews and articles.

Any resemblance to persons alive or dead is purely coincidental.

Cover by Lily Bear Design Co.

Edited by Victoria Ellis of Cruel Ink Publishing.

Proofread by Beth Hale of Magnolia Publishing.

Formatted by Shannon O'Connor.

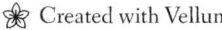

SHANNON O'CONNOR

To all the girls who never quite felt like a "Barbie" growing up but played with them anyway.

Doll Face
Playlist

Nonsense - Sabrina Carpenter
Sit Still, Look Pretty - Daya
Another Life - Surf Mesa, Joshua Golden, FLETCHER
Mother - Meghan Trainor
The Sound - The 1975
Kiss You - One Direction
Gorgeous - Taylor Swift
No One Compares to You - Jack & Jack
Shower - Becky G
Starving - Hailee Steinfeld, Grey, Zedd
Cherry - FLETCHER, Hayley Kiyoko

Chapter 1

Barbie

"Come on, Doll Face, you know this will happen again." Kenzie smirks from the bed, lying under a thin, pink sheet.

"You know I hate it when you call me that," I grumble.

"But it's true. And you are built like a doll, *Barbie*." She laughs at her own joke. At times like this, I hate my name. But that's what you get when two toymakers have a blonde daughter together—they name her *Barbie*.

"Anyway. This was *fun* but you should really get going." I stand with my hands on my hips. Although, I know I can't be that intimidating while completely naked.

"Barbie, look. I'm sorry I didn't tell you about the trip but I need you to come back to bed," Kenzie begs. She had conveniently forgotten to mention that she was leaving late tonight on a red eye out of California and heading straight for London. She hasn't even mentioned how long she'll be gone for.

"Why?" I pout.

"Because we deserve to leave things on a high note. This isn't goodbye, it's just see you later," she assures me.

I walk back to the bed and climb underneath the sheets as I make a face, pushing out my bright pink lipstick stained lips at her.

"Barbie, you know I love you, right?"

"I do." I nod. "And I love you, too."

"Then will you make love to me before I have to go?" Kenzie smiles. "Or we can both lie here and watch a movie or something."

"Oh, just kiss me already." I roll my eyes. Kenzie closes the distance with her shiny, red lips on mine and we kiss. Her tongue dances across my mouth, sliding in perfectly and causing me to moan in anticipation.

"Mmm," she whimpers as I reach for her breasts. They are bigger and perkier than mine, an asset she has on display often.

"I want you," I mutter against her.

"Fuck me, Barbie," she whispers my name, and I feel my pussy getting wetter and wetter. I love it when she says my name.

Kenzie's body isn't a typical model's body. She isn't all abs and hardness, and she doesn't stick to a strict diet like so many others in her profession. Kenzie is technically a plus-size model but the industry is finally getting away from using the outdated term. She's just a model who can eat what she wants and show off her body. It's rather impressive. It's not like my body isn't. I'm tall and thin and blonde, and some people joke that I look like my namesake. I love everything about Kenzie's body. Her curves and the way her body is soft and squishy. Her body is one of the first things I noticed about her, which I know might sound a little shallow, but she was half naked during a photo shoot that I happened to drop in on. Her breasts were on full display, along with her stomach, and she came up to me without a care in the world. I did my best to keep eye contact with her, and she invited herself to lunch with the photographer and me. It was history from there; even fully clothed she was beautiful, and I couldn't keep my eyes off her. It was one of those love at first sight occurrences. Thankfully, she felt the same.

"Where'd you just go?" Kenzie asks before kissing my neck.

"I was thinking about how we met actually." I smile.

"You were incredible. I've never seen someone work so hard to keep eye contact. I thought you might've been straight." She laughs.

"It's one of the hardest things I've ever done," I tease.

"I have something easy for you to do." She wiggles her dark eyebrows, and I blush. I know what she's insinuating.

"You want to?" It's one of my favorite ways to have an orgasm, but I know it's not her first choice.

"I want to." She nods. Then, she lies down, and I climb on top of her, one leg between her thighs and the other on the side of her hips.

Bending down, I kiss her again. This time with more ferocity. I want her, and I need her to know just how much. My hands roam her body, stopping at her delicious breasts and lingering at her nipples. I take one between my thumb and finger, gingerly pinching it and watching her moan beneath me.

"Oh, baby," she murmurs.

"You like that?" I smile, already knowing the answer.

"Mmm," she whimpers.

I slide my hands around her curves, taking a moment to touch every inch of her before my hand finds her core. She's actually dripping for me, something I will never get tired of seeing or feeling. I want to taste her but this isn't the time. She wants to scissor, and fuck if I will let this occasion go to waste. I slide my fingers up and down her core a few times, wetting her clit and covering my fingers in her juices. Then I look Kenzie straight in the eye and suck my fingers clean; one taste won't hurt. I can't resist tasting her sweet pussy.

"Fuck me already, baby," she commands, and I nod.

Positioning my core over hers, I hold her leg in the air and begin to rock my hips against hers. The second our clits touch, we both let out a primal moan. Thankfully, we have the place to ourselves, and there's no one nearby to hear us. I hold her deliciously thick thighs in place while I ride on top of her. Kenzie's shaking her hips, too, meeting each motion with her own. I'm too close to a release in this position. Something about doing it like this always makes me come in a matter of minutes.

"Fuck me baby," Kenzie moans out.

"Oh, I'm so close."

"Come for me, baby. Come like a good little slut," she commands. The word *slut* is what pushes me over the edge—her dirty mouth will be the death of me.

"Oh, Kenzie! Fuuuuuck!" I call out. I keep my hips moving until my legs give out under me.

"Fuck." She smiles at me while I collapse next to her.

"You didn't ..."

She shakes her head. "Perfect," I say mischievously, and when I gain enough energy, I crawl to the edge of the bed, get down on my knees, and pull her pussy into my face.

"Oh, Barbie, you don't have to ... Oh!" She stops herself when I press my tongue to her clit. I know I don't *have* to, but I'm about to show her how much I *want* to.

I lap my tongue up and down her folds, sopping up as much of her wetness as I possibly can. She whimpers under me, biting down on her beautiful red lips. She tries to suppress her moans. It's cute how she thinks she has any ounce of control. I press my tongue against her core and watch as she bucks her hips and screams out for me. All I ever need to do is press my tongue against her, and she's putty in my hands.

Or on my tongue.

Sliding two fingers inside of her, I stretch out her tight pussy and pump in and out while she calls out for me. Her hips begin to buck, and she starts to ride my hand while I lick around her clit. Then I stop to tease her, sucking and kissing on the insides of her thighs. I love giving her a taste of her own medicine, and from the way she's moaning, I know she loves it too. No matter how much she might complain later.

"I'm close!" she whimpers out.

"Don't come yet," I say, pausing from my feast.

"W-what?" She looks at me with pained eyes.

"I want you to wait. I want you to come but not until I allow it. I'm not done tasting you," I say against her. Blowing lightly on her core, I smile as she gasps, and her breathing picks up. I can tell she's trying so hard not to come despite how much her body wants her to let go.

I continue eating her out, tasting every last drop of her deliciousness and watching as she's struggling to hold on. I give her one last lick and then purr against her core.

"Come for me," I command, and she lights up like the fucking Fourth of July. Her body raises off the bed, and she moans for me. Her legs thrash for a second, and then she's catching her breath and clenching her jaw.

"Fuck, no one does it like you do." She smiles.

"They better not," I grumble.

"Oh trust me, I will be thinking about that orgasm all night long." She laughs.

I lie down next to her in bed and let her pull me into her arms for a cuddle. She spoons me and starts playing with my hair.

"I love you, Doll Face," Kenzie whispers in my ear.

"I love you too," I whisper back with a yawn. A wave of sleepiness rushes over me, and my eyes begin to close. I'm no match for the post-orgasm sleepiness I feel. So, within a matter of minutes, I'm out cold.

When I wake, I'm alone. Kenzie's spot in bed is still warm but she's nowhere to be found. I walk around the house looking for her. Calling out her name and looking in each of the rooms, I realize she's nowhere to be found. When I return to bed, I notice a note on her nightstand that's folded in pink paper. *Was that there earlier?*

Barbie,

I couldn't bear to wake you. You looked so peaceful, and I didn't want to fight again. I'll call you when I get to London. I love you.

Love,

Kenzie

SHE EVEN LEFT a red lipstick print at the bottom next to her name. I'm upset she didn't wake me to say goodbye but it's probably for the best. We're both too emotional when it comes to goodbyes. Last time we had to say goodbye, both of us ended up sobbing at the airport, and she probably wanted to avoid that—I get it. I just wish I had a chance to see her again before she left. Sure, she's only going for a few weeks, but that's still a long ass time to go without seeing the woman you love.

Chapter 2

Barbie

5 years later...

"I needed those designs on my desk over an hour ago! Where could they be?" I shout to no one in particular. I'm about to lose my mind, so I take a deep breath in and out before looking at my assistant.

"Can you please go grab me a pink drink? I need a large one if I'm going to be working all night," I say to my redheaded assistant, Midge. I'm not much of a coffee drinker but I love the Pink Drink from Starbucks—mainly because they're full of caffeine.

"Yes, ma'am. And I think the designs are still with Kelly," she says before leaving.

Kelly is my next in line. Whenever I *do* take a day off, she's in charge. Trusting her with the company is easy—she's my blood, after all. My little sister knows how important my job is to me. When our parents left Up, Up, Away toys to me, they didn't anticipate that toys would take a backseat to tablets and other electronics. We're competitive in the toy business, ranking high enough to sit at the table with Mattel and others, but that still doesn't mean I can take a day off to relax like my sister can. I have too much riding on making sure the family business doesn't crumble. It's all on my shoulders, and I don't want to let my parents down.

"Can someone get Kelly down here?" I ask my string of interns. They look up from their computers, then at each other, and one of them picks up the phone.

"She's coming down now," they say, hanging up the phone.

"Good." I look down at the half-assed papers in front of me. They won't be complete until we get the designs from Kelly. The next quarter of sales depends on these designs, and I have to make sure they're going to bring in enough revenue to keep us afloat. It's been a rough few years; despite being competitive, we still aren't doing as well as Apple or Amazon.

"What's up, sis?" Kelly walks in the room wearing wheelie sneakers and a pair of ripped jeans. Thank GOD for casual Fridays.

"I need the Woods designs for the toy line." I sigh.

"Got them right here. I was going over logistics with the team," she says, proudly rolling over to me.

"Thank you." I take them from her and look them over. If we can create this exact line, and in time for Christmas, we'll be under our yearly budget.

"They look good, right?" she asks, searching for my approval.

"They look amazing. Did you help?" She's more on the administrative side of things, but I've known of her to dip her toes in the designs every once in a while. We need her as our CFO, but if we didn't, she'd be head of the design department. She's surely talented enough for the position.

"I did. I know you said not to, but I couldn't help myself. I'm the one who did that one." She points to one of my favorite toys.

"It looks really amazing." I smile.

"Thanks." She grins.

Just then, Midge comes back with my Pink Drink in her hand. My eyes light up when I see it, and I take it from her with a quick thank you. She checks if I need anything else, and when I don't, she heads back to her desk outside the conference room.

"Mom and Dad called, by the way. They're wondering if you're vacationing with us in Hawaii. We leave in like two days, you know."

"I know; they've left me messages. I just don't think I can swing it with both of us not being here," I admit. If Kelly were staying home, I'd consider it, but I'm a workaholic who would probably stick around anyway.

"I told them you'd say that." She shakes her head. "Will you be okay here without me?"

"I'll be fine."

"You should get out more, you know. Go on a date. See the city. Be spontaneous."

"I've lived in New York for four and a half years; I know the city." I laugh.

"Well, you should get out and date more."

I turn toward the batch of interns. "Excuse us a minute?" They all trickle out of the office, and I turn back to Kelly. "Where is all this coming from?"

"Mom and dad are just worried about you. And so am I. You work so much. But you never go out ... you never date. You haven't dated anyone since Kenzie." She never brings her up, so I know she must actually be concerned.

"Fine. I'll grab a drink with someone. I'll have a night out and potentially meet someone, but you really don't have to worry about me. I'm okay, even without Kenzie." I try not to wince while saying her name. It's like saying it out loud makes me realize how much I actually miss her.

Kenzie left for London five years ago and never came back. She took a modeling job there, and sure, we tried long distance at first, but that inevitably fizzled out. We lost contact and that was the end of the person I thought I was going to spend the rest of my life with. So I understand and appreciate my family's concern, but it's also pointless for me to date when I'm still healing. I'm not entirely over Kenzie, and I honestly don't know if I'll ever be.

"It's okay to not be okay, Babs," my sister says, using her special nickname for me.

"I know." I nod. I hate talking about this. It's bringing forth all this emotion that I would much rather keep inside.

"I'll drop it, but promise you'll at least try to go out? Wear that new pink dress you bought last year that hangs in your closet."

"I think that's a little too much for a date." I laugh. Pink is my favorite color, and I wear it most days to the office anyway.

I used to dress more "professional." I opted for tans and neutrals but it was actually making me depressed. So, since then, I've been getting tailor-made pink business attire. If people are going to joke about me looking like a Barbie doll, I might as well lean into it. There's no harm in dressing up how I like, and besides, I'm wearing office attire. It's just a bit more pink than traditional business clothing.

"No, it's so *you*," she says, still talking about my dress. I consider it for a moment. I mean, maybe she has a point.

"Maybe." I can always think about it later. Am I really going to go out tonight? I know Kelly will check up on it tomorrow, and I'm not exactly the best liar.

"Barbie!" Midge calls, opening the door. She's not normally one to interrupt us.

"What's going on?"

"Kelly, you better come too, there's been a problem in manufacturing." Midge looks panicked.

"What kind of problem?" Kelly asks.

"It's best if you see for yourself." Midge looks at the ground and bites her bottom lip. It's something bad alright; I've never seen her look so nervous before.

We walk down the hallway and take the elevator to manufacturing—a place Kelly and I rarely circle. We trust our employees and never want to be those bosses that randomly check up on things ... unless we have to. This feels like walking down the hall to the principal's office. A row of employees watches our every move. With the click-clack of my pink heels, I feel like I'm walking into an execution.

"So? Someone want to tell me what's going on?" I prompt one of the engineers.

"Well, it seems like we got in the wrong mold, and no one checked it prior to starting assembly. Now we have over a thousand of them, and we don't know what to do with it," he says sheepishly.

"One thousand what?" I spit out. *How didn't anyone check the mold? What the hell are they doing down here?*

"Umm." He falters. "These, ma'am." He holds up one bright pink penis-shaped dildo, and my eyes widen.

"Oh, my God!" Kelly exclaims, and I shoot her a look.

"It seems a sex toy company has a similar name to ours, and they got our mold. They're sending it over now but we, uh, didn't know what to do with these," the guy says.

My brain immediately goes into thinking mode. "Are they usable?"

"Ma'am?" He blushes.

"I'm asking if they can be used for their intended purpose with the materials they were processed with?" I'm trying to be professional about this.

"Well...yes." He hesitates.

"So, what we're going to do is send some up to marketing and have them come up with how we can sell them for the holiday season."

"Are you serious?" Kelly laughs.

"I'm dead serious. Otherwise we're out a shit ton of money and materials, and for what?"

"We could always contact the sex toy company and sell it to them?"

"I like that idea even better. Kelly, run point on this. I don't want to hear about these toys until they're producing a profit for us."

"You got it." Kelly nods. "Get all of them in one spot, and I'll get in contact with that other company."

"Why would a sex toy company be called 'Up, Up, Away' anyway?" I ask, confused, and that's when the man starts laughing uncontrollably.

"It's actually called Up, Up, & Anal, ma'am," he says after he gets himself under control.

"Well, that makes a lot more sense. Just make sure it doesn't happen again," I instruct. Kelly begins asking for the company's number, and I leave her to fix the rest.

Midge follows me back to the office. For the rest of the day, there aren't any other issues, thankfully. I do my budgeting and paperwork in my office alone before heading home for the night. It's just after five when I'm headed out of the building. Midge is cleaning up her desk when I say goodnight. I head for the elevator and text Kelly about the dildo issue. I hope she's figured out a solution to our big, pink problem. It isn't like we can just put them on the shelves next to the toy bears and stuffed Disney toys.

There's no service in the elevator so I slip my phone in my bag and wait to get to the lobby. Maybe I'll grab sushi on the way home from work. I can even pick up a bottle of champagne. I know it's usually saved for celebrations but I want to pop a bottle, slip into the tub, and call it a day.

I'm walking out the front steps of the building when my phone starts ringing. It could be work calling me back in. It wouldn't be the first time that's happened. Or, it could be Kelly. I decide to search through my bag as I walk, just in case it's important.

"Whoa!" I bump into someone, almost dropping my bag and its contents all over the ground. I look up and shock runs through my body.

"Barbie." Kenzie smiles at me. Her brunette hair is pulled into a tight ponytail, and she's wearing a black dress that hugs her curves. My eyes trail all the way down her body and I note a pair of heels that put mine to shame.

"Kenzie? W-what are you doing here?" I ask, confused. A shiver runs down my spine, and I'm hit with a wave of nostalgia as the former love of my life stands only inches away from me.

Chapter 3

Kenzie

I got off the plane, and despite the list of places I was supposed to go to, I stop at Up, Up, Away toy company headquarters. The only person I want to see is about a million floors away from me, and I'm pretty sure I still remember which one she's on. She's head of the company, and I don't know how hard it'll be to get to the top floor, but I'm prepared for anything. Just as I'm about to run inside and try and find Barbie, I see her walking out of the elevator. She's in an all pink suit, her shiny, pink purse reflects on the doors, and her bright pink heels clack as she walks. She's as beautiful as ever—a true doll.

I'm about to make my move when I realize she's not looking where she's going, and she ends up bumping into me.

"Barbie." I smile, steadying her.

"Kenzie? W-what are you doing here?" she asks.

"I'm in town, and I had to find you," I explain.

"Why?" She looks around like she's on a prank show or something. Like someone's about to pop out of a fake cake.

"I've missed you," I say simply. I know it can't possibly be enough, but it has to be a start.

"Kenzie ..." she starts but doesn't finish.

"Can I take you out to dinner? We can catch up, talk about things, maybe see where we both are in life?" I suggest with a smile.

"No," she says sharply. I should've expected that but her refusal slices through me.

"Oh." I sigh.

"I better go." She tries to sidestep me but I hold out an arm to stop her.

"Barbie—"

She shakes her head and looks at me, holding up her palm as her blue eyes stare into mine.

"I-I can't, Kenzie. I just can't." She takes off, hailing a cab and leaving without another word or look in my direction.

I stand on the steps of her building feeling defeated, but only for a moment. Barbie has no idea I've got an entire week left in this city. I have another six days to convince her to sit down with me. My main goal is to talk everything out, but maybe I'll even get her to agree to start slowly incorporating me back into her life. I know she isn't seeing anyone, at least not according to her Instagram ...

I may have been stalking her social media over the last few weeks.

Conceding defeat for the night, I retreat to my hotel across town. I had opted for a hotel closer to Barbie's job, but my booking got cancelled at the last minute. I know, I know, anyone else might look at that as a sign, but not me. I know what Barbie and I had, and although it might be over for now, it was years in the making. I refuse to let it go. I know I wasn't around the last few years but I never forgot about her or what we had together.

"What's got you in a slump?" my best friend, Ken, asks. He's as gay as I am, and a male model, one I'm often paired with for shoots. Over the years, we've bonded and become close—so much so that I feel like I know him better than almost anyone else.

Ken and Kenzie, BFFs for life.

"I just saw Barbie," I explain.

"And I'm assuming she wasn't exactly excited to see you?"

"No, not at all." I sigh.

"Well, at least you tried." He hands me a bottle of water, and I take a long sip.

"I'm not done yet," I say, determined.

He raises an eyebrow. "You're ... not?"

"I'm going to try again tomorrow and the next day and everyday we're here until she talks to me."

Ken stays quiet. I know what he's thinking.

"Look, if she really wants me to stay away from her, then I will; I'm not some crazy ass stalker. But I can't give up without trying my hardest for her," I say.

"Then you must have some kind of plan."

"I'm going to stop by her job tomorrow with roses and hope that she'll talk to me." It doesn't feel like much of a plan but it is enough of a start.

"Well, as long you're doing what you think is best. You know her better than anyone."

"I hope you're right."

THE NEXT MORNING, I head to Barbie's job and sweet talk her doorman into allowing me to deliver the bouquet of pink roses, her favorite, in person. He is sweet, and once I start talking about true love, he buzzes me up with no problem. It is quite unsafe, but hey, it isn't like I am going to murder her if she refuses to be with me.

I'm walking down the hallway of offices when I spot a pink one at the end of the hall. There are clear glass doors, and I see a few people, but not the one woman I want to see.

"Hi, I'm here to see Barbie." I smile politely to the frazzled redhead at the desk in front of her office. I'm assuming it's her assistant.

"She's not in yet," she says.

"Can I wait? It's important I get these flowers to her."

"Wow, a delivery woman who makes sure the flowers get delivered? You can sit right there; I'm sure she should be here any minute now." The woman smiles. I don't correct her or tell her who I am, just in case she's heard of me.

Five minutes later, the elevator doors open, and Barbie walks down the hall in her pink heels. She's wearing a long pink coat, a pink blouse, and a light pink skirt. She looks like CEO Barbie. I crack a smile. I always knew she was destined for a position like this. Her face falls when she sees me.

"W-what are you doing here?" She turns to the redhead. "What is she doing here?"

"She said she was here to deliver flowers," she says nervously.

"I didn't tell her who I was," I say. I don't want anyone getting fired or into trouble because of me.

"Midge, call security. This is my ex-girlfriend," she says with a deadpan expression, staring at me. Midge looks at me with wide eyes and goes to pick up the phone.

"Barbie, come on, just talk to me." I hold out the bouquet of flowers, and she looks at them and then back at me.

"I don't know what you want to talk about." She crosses her arms over her chest.

"Can we talk in private?" I eye Midge, and she's holding the phone up to her ear while looking between us.

"Fine, come in my office." Barbie sighs.

"So am I calling security?" Midge asks, and I look to Barbie who shakes her head in defeat.

"Isn't this office a little *not so* private?" I motion toward the see-through doors.

"It's completely soundproof. Someone could scream and Midge wouldn't hear it." She slides her coat off and takes a seat. Her desk is light rose gold complete with the rose gold Mac.

"That's comforting," I mumble.

"I'm not the one who left, Kenzie. Also, relax. I'm not the murdering type. Orange isn't my color." Barbie cracks a smile, and I can't help but laugh.

"I just want to talk about us." I sit down across from her.

"There is no *us*."

"Barbie—" I'm about to go into why there *is* an us when we're interrupted by another blonde. She waltzes right in like she owns the place and drops a file on Barbie's desk. Her eyes finally meet mine, and realization flashes through her features at the same time I recognize her.

"Oh my gosh! Kenzie?" It's Barbie's younger sister,

Kelly, except she's no longer a teenager with braces; she's basically all grown up.

"Hey, Kelly." I smile. She comes over and greets me with a hug.

"When I said get back out there, this isn't exactly what I meant, but I'm all for this." Kelly winks at Barbie.

"Kelly! We're in the middle of something," Barbie scolds.

"Whoops! Well, I'm glad to see you back together. Mom and Dad will be so happy."

"We're n—" I start to say, but Barbie cuts me off.

"Let me be the one to tell them the good news." Barbie forces a smile.

"Okay, okay." Kelly groans. "I still can't believe this. You two work fast." She smiles. "See you around, Kenzie."

"What just happened?" I look at Barbie, confused.

"My sister is on my case to get back out there and date someone. So are my parents, so I'm just telling them what they want to hear," she says with a shrug.

"So we're not getting back together?" I ask, scrunching my eyebrows.

"Kenzie, you can't come back after four and a half years and expect me to jump back into something with you. That's seriously insane."

"So give me a week."

"W-what?"

"Give me a week to show you that we belong together, and if at the end of the week you're not convinced, I'll go willingly and leave you alone."

"Why a week?"

"That's how long I'm in town for."

"So a week to get you out of my life, then?" she asks, full of sass.

"Sure, you can think of it like that."

"Fine." She nods.

"We have a deal." I reach forward to shake her manicured hand and smile. This wouldn't be easy but I know I'll be able to do it. All I have to do is remind her of all the good parts of us. Surely it won't be that hard to do.

I step out of her office, confident that I can do just that. I know what we had all those years ago was special. But I was young and dumb and threw it all away for my career. Not that I regret that, but I wish I hadn't had to choose between the two. I'm getting older, and I miss being with Barbie more than anything.

I text Ken and let him know I'm on my way back, and I head to the photo shoot. I'm not sure what the shoot is for but I know my agent wants me to be there with a big smile on my face. According to the fashion world, I'm getting older, and even for a plus-size model, my career will be changing soon. I'll become the mother in the shoot instead of the main attraction, and sure, that's weighing on me, but it's also a little bit of a relief. I'll be able to hang in the back of the shoot and not be the main attraction—something I thought I'd never get over being.

Sometimes I can't help but wonder what my life would've been like had I not taken the modeling job that ended my relationship with Barbie. Would we still be together? Would we have broken up anyway? This is my second chance. This is my way to rewrite our history, and I'm not about to lose my chance. I knew being sent to New York after so many years in London was a sign. What kind of sign? A sign that I had to give it another go with Barbie. Even if it changes everything for me. She's beyond worth it.

Arriving at the shoot, I find Ken already dressed and all done up. I'm not late. Ken just likes to be early for everything. I plop my butt into the chair and scroll through my phone as the makeup artist does wonders on my skin. I'm about to check in on Barbie's page again when I get a notification.

*You have **1** new follower.*

I CLICK on the link and butterflies float through my chest. Barbie is now "following" me. Maybe this actually is the start of something brand-new. As much as I enjoy thinking about my past with Barbie, maybe I'd be better off approaching this as something brand-new. I should try to get to know her as the person she is now and see if our feelings are still there. Seeing her again didn't change anything for me, but I know I still have some convincing to do on her part.

Chapter 4

Barbie

Now that Kenzie has left me alone, I have way too much time to think. Of course it was Kelly who had to barge in and ask if we're back together. But why didn't I just deny it? Something about Kelly and my parents being on my case about who I'm dating lately made me want to show them I'm not as lonely as I seem.

That I'm not lonely at all.

But of course Kenzie thinks she has a chance with me now, and I don't know what to do about that. My head is spinning, so I open my door and ask Midge to run and get me a Pink Drink from downstairs. I can barely focus on paperwork or anything adjacent.

"Here you go." Midge comes back a few minutes later with my drink. I smile and take a hearty sip. She heads back to her desk, and I think about Kenzie.

I pull out my phone and decide to look at her Instagram. It's the same handle it used to be, and don't ask me why I remember, but I do, so I find her profile easily. She has thousands of followers, and many of her posts are about her modeling shoots. She's in her underwear a lot, which only turns me on. I love how body positive her page is. She doesn't hide any of her curves or stretch marks, and it's easy to tell that none of her pictures are edited. She's authentically herself. I don't overthink it, and before I know what I'm doing, I'm hitting the *follow* button. I mean, I need some way to contact her, don't I? She follows me back almost immediately, and I grin.

I set my phone down and try to get some actual work done to no avail. I'm about to give up for the morning when Kelly comes in my office again.

"I'm going to put a bell on you, I swear," I say. Kelly is always barging in without so much as even a quick knock.

"Your doors are see through, you can see me coming." She shrugs and takes a seat across from me.

"What do you need?" I ask with a sigh.

"I need a favor! And you still owe me for not telling Mom and Dad about you and Kenzie."

"Okay." I groan and roll my eyes. "How could I ever forget?"

"I was supposed to go to this charity auction tomorrow, but I'm headed to Hawaii with Mom and Dad, so I was hoping you'd go in my place?" She smiles, showing all of her pearly-white teeth.

"Do I have to?" I wince. Going to these kinds of things alone makes me a target for the rich and single, and I hate it.

"There's an open bar, and I said we'd donate a basket of toys for their auction."

"Oh." I sigh.

"Pleaseeeeee?" She elongates the word and gives me her best puppy dog eyes.

"Yeah, that's fine. Send Midge all the information, and I'll be there." I give in.

"Really?!" she asks, clearly excited.

Doll Face

"Yes." I nod.

"Perfect!" She beams like she's up to something but I'm too afraid to ask.

"I'll be sure to go in your place." I smile. I like going to events like this—when I'm *not* alone—especially ones I can dress up for and donate money to. It's part of why I don't currently have a millionaire status, but I am a big supporter of giving back whenever I can. I mean, why do I need so much money, anyway?

"Thank you! You're the best!" She blows me a kiss with her hand and heads out of my office—but I'm sure it won't be the last time I see her today.

I pull out my phone and see a message from Kenzie on Instagram.

> Kenzie: What are you doing tomorrow? Hint: Giving me a chance to show you all you've been missing … 😉

> Barbie: 😍😍😍

> Kenzie: Keep those eyes on me, baby.

> Kenzie: *Barbie

I LAUGH OUT LOUD. I forgot how much of a flirt Kenzie could be.

> Kenzie: Here's my number. I'm above sliding in your DMs.

I SAVE her number in my phone with a sassy-faced emoji and text her a simple pink heart; she'll know who it's from. Almost immediately, she calls me.

"Hello?" I ask, confused.

"Thank God. We're too old to be flirting in each other's DMs," she says with a laugh.

"Excuse me? I wasn't flirting," I say sharply.

"Not yet, but you were just about to." I roll my eyes but I realize she can't see that.

"I can hear those eyes rolling to the back of your head and hitting your beautiful brain, Doll Face," she says, and the old nickname hits me where it hurts.

"I hate how well you know me," I mumble.

"I love how much you haven't changed."

"I have."

"You're still just as stubborn." She laughs.

"Did you call just call me stubborn?" I cross my hands over my chest. Not that I want the phone call to end, but I am curious why she's calling in general.

"Is it cheesy if I say I've missed your voice?"

"Yes."

"Good. I've missed your voice," she says.

"Gross." I'm glad she can't see the grin I'm sporting.

"I can almost hear a smile forming, Doll Face. Don't be such a grump. When am I seeing you again?"

"Four days from never." I put the phone in the crook of my shoulder and ear so I can look at my calendar. I'm curious if I'm busy the next few days, *just in case.*

"Barbie ..." She sighs.

"Kenzie?"

"Don't make plans this week. I'll surprise you. But right now I have to get back to work. Have a great day, Doll Face."

"Bye, Kenzie." She ends the call before I can, and I think about her voice. Her laugh. How nice it was to hear from her again. I thought she was joking about using this week to prove things to me but maybe she was serious.

THE NEXT NIGHT, I'm getting ready for the ball by myself, and I can't help but feel a little lonely. Usually Kelly and I get ready for things like this together, but she's on a plane to Hawaii, and I don't even have a date.

The thought causes Kenzie to pop into my brain, and I wonder what she's up to tonight. Not that I would ask her to join me for something like this, but I'm just curious. I know I shouldn't be, but it's like stalking your exes on social media—I can't help it.

I think about the last time I was at one of these events with Kenzie. It was back when we were still living in California, and she was meeting my parents for the first time. It was a fundraiser for Up, Up, Away and some charity I can't remember the name of. But I do remember that night clearer than anything.

"ARE you sure they're going to like me?" Kenzie asks again.

"I'm positive." I smile, fixing her necklace.

"But what if they don't?"

"I don't think I've ever seen you so nervous before. It's adorably cute."

"It is not. I've never met someone's parents before. I'm like, freaking out. I'm going to sweat through my dress." She fans her armpits.

"It's just a fundraiser for charity. They aren't going to make a scene at a work event, and besides, they're going to love you. I know I do."

"Yeah? Say that again." She smiles.

"I love you, Kenzie."

"I love you, too." She kisses me chastely, careful not to smudge our lipstick.

We head to the event together, and I don't tell her I'm just as nervous as she is. What if my parents don't like her? Kelly had already met her but she's fairly easy to please. She's just a teenager. Mom and Dad are different. They are trusting me with so much responsibility at work lately, and what if they thought I shouldn't be bringing anyone home right now or something? What-if they don't like that she's a lingerie model? Will it make a difference to me if they tell me not to see her or something? No. I'm in love with Kenzie, and although we've only been dating a few months, it feels like the real deal.

"Okay, here we go." Kenzie takes a deep breath as we arrive at the fundraiser.

"You got this." I beam, reminding her it'll be okay. I'm partially reminding myself, too.

"Don't leave my side, okay?"

"Promise." I nod.

The place is decorated to the nines, and I can tell my mother had something to do with it. While my signature color is pink, hers is red—and this entire place screams of her.

There are red and gold decorations everywhere, and the tables are colored red to match. It's a little bit of an overkill, but everything looks nice together. The place is packed, and I know we need to find my parents before they start making speeches and things. Kenzie and I have only planned to make an appearance, meet my parents, and then take Kelly home with us. It's too long of an event to keep a teenager occupied, and my parents want an eye on Kelly at all times. She's a bit of a wild child if not kept on a tight leash. But then again, who isn't at her age?

"Do you see them anywhere?" Kenzie asks, as I look around the room.

"Nope." I frown.

"Barbie!" I hear my name being called. Kelly's dodging her way across the room to us. "Thank goodness you're here, can we go now? I'm so bored."

"We just got here, we have to say hello to Mom and Dad."

"Hey, Kenzie. You look nervous," Kelly points out.

"Kelly!" I scold my sister. She's going to make Kenzie even more nervous.

"I do?"

"No, you look fine. Kelly, go talk to someone your age, and I'll find you in a bit, okay?"

"Fine," she grumbles and takes off toward the buffet table.

"Do I really look nervous?" Kenzie asks, wide-eyed.

"No, you look beautiful." I look around the room again and find my mom, which means my dad shouldn't be too far behind. "Come on." I take Kenzie by the hand and lead her over to my parents.

My mom is talking to someone and using her fake smile, pretending to be interested in the story. It looks artificial, *especially with all the plastic surgery she's had over the years, but if you weren't her daughter, you'd probably think it was a genuine grin. She spots me and excuses herself, pulling my dad along with her until she reaches me and gives me a big hug.*

"Hi, sweetheart." She sports a fake grin.

"Hey, Mom," I greet her. "Hi, Dad." I smile.

"Hello there, sweetie." He hugs me too.

"Mom, Dad, this is my girlfriend, Kenzie." I introduce them and they both shake her hand.

"It's nice to meet you both, Barbie's said so many nice things about you."

"She's had the kindest things to say about you, too. You make our daughter very happy," my mom says.

"I try," Kenzie says sheepishly. "She makes me very happy, too."

"Young love is something you should hold onto; it's a rare thing," my dad adds and looks at my mom adoringly. They've been married since they were both eighteen and they have the best marriage I've ever seen. It's something I hope to have for myself one day.

"Got it, sir." She looks at me, causing me to blush.

"Why don't you go save your sister from the buffet and take her home? I know she doesn't want to be here, and you two shouldn't be subjected to a boring work fundraiser," Mom says.

"Are you sure?" I ask.

"I'm sure, it'll be your time to do this soon enough." My mom winks.

I SNAP out of the memory, thinking about how simple it was to introduce Kenzie to my parents and how much they liked her from that moment on. She was eventually invited to all of our family gatherings, and my parents asked about her a lot after we broke up. I always felt like they missed her just as much as I did after Kenzie left. It was like she had become a bonus family member that was ripped away from all of us.

Chapter 5

Kenzie

"Kelly?" I pick up my phone and look at the caller ID, wondering if the contact is still correct. It's been years since she called me.

"Yup! Wow, you still have my number? That's so sweet!" she says, practically gushing.

"What can I do for you?"

"I was hoping you could accompany my sister to a charity ball tomorrow night."

"What? Does Barbie have any idea that you're calling and asking me this right now?"

"Nope! And you're not going to tell her." She giggles. God, I forgot how mischievous her sister could be.

"Why wouldn't I tell her?"

"Because you want to take her to this ball. I don't know what's going on between the two of you but I can tell you want to take her. Don't make me ask someone else," she threatens.

"Alright, you got a deal."

"Just don't tell her you're going or she might ... umm ... back out."

"Jesus. Sure. So am I sneaking into this thing, too?"

"Well, no. I'll leave your ticket at the box office under Campbell."

Barbie and Kelly's last name. I remember that easily; it had almost been my last name.

"Okay."

"And wear something nice! You'll want to dress to impress."

"You do realize I'm a model, right? Dressing to impress is literally my job." I laugh.

"Right. Brain fart! Anyway! Hope you two have a fun time," she says and hangs up before I can ask anything else. She texts me an address a moment later, and I add it to my map app for tomorrow.

"What's going on?" Ken asks, walking over.

"I'm apparently taking Barbie to a ball," I say.

"Oh? She just asked you out of the blue?" he asks.

"No, her sister actually set the whole thing up."

"Wow." He pauses. "Wait, so Barbie has no idea?"

"No, I don't think so."

"That's going to be interesting." He chuckles.

"Is the shoot over? We need to go find me a dress."

He nods. "Yup, they said they just need some shots of Melanie and Tori, so we're both done for the day." He smiles. I have on heavy, evening makeup and Ken's hair is sprayed to the gods, but that won't stop us from going to a few stores and trying on outfits.

We change into casual clothes, which for me is a pair of jeans and a crop top. I grab my bag and wait for Ken to change before we leave. I'm not familiar with New York City boutiques, but I'm about to be. We take an Uber to Fifth Avenue and head to the shops there. I need a dress—and fast—and that's not always easy for someone my size.

The first two stores we try are a total miss. I was turned away after asking if they sold anything above a size eight. I'm a proud size eighteen, and on some days a twenty. I'm not about to waste my time looking in stores that don't have my body size on display. We hit the third store, and when I see a more shapely looking display model, I know we've come to the right place.

"Excuse me, where can I find your ball gowns? Preferably in a size eighteen?" I ask one of the saleswomen.

"We keep them all to the left, but they make us keep anything above a size fourteen in the back," one of the women says with an eye roll. She's similar in size to me, so I know she understands how frustrating it must be to work in a store that does that.

"Would you be able to pull a few in size eighteen? I definitely want to try some on."

"Of course! Any color or style in particular?"

"I prefer darker colors. Definitely nothing pink. I have a feeling that's the color my date will be wearing," I say with a smile. I'm sure my girl has already chosen a beautiful, pink dress to wear for the event.

"Okay, you can wait over there by the dressing rooms. I will bring some over." She nods and heads into the back.

"We're in 2023 and they're still keeping your size in the back? When will they open their eyes and see most of America wears bigger than a size two?" Ken grumbles. He knows all about my rage when it comes to beauty standards. We've been on too many shoots where I was referred to as a "plus-size" model instead of just a model. It's frustrating as hell but I'm not going to take it out on the workers who are just following company policy.

"I'm sadly used to it. I'm just glad they have something in my size. I didn't want to have to go ask another store," I

It's hard walking up to thinner women who don't understand my struggle.

"You shouldn't *have* to go to another store," Ken says with a sigh.

"Here you are." The woman comes out with a rack full of dresses for me to try on. Since they're so big and bulky it looks like a lot, but in reality, there's only about five dresses. Most of them are black, one is navy, and one is tan. I paw through one side while Ken looks at the other side. The first three don't really do it for me but then Ken pulls out a strapless black one, and we both have the same thought.

"It would look fantastic on you." He claps.

"I'd like to try it on," I say. I don't want to get attached to a dress that turns out to be lumpy in all the wrong places. I don't enjoy wearing Spanx or any other gut-sucking-in material. Praise to the women who can, but for me it sucks in too much of my belly; it hurts like a bitch. I let everything hang naturally, which means, depending on the dress, there could be some unnatural lumps.

"Here you go!" The woman opens one of the dressing rooms and hands me the dress on the hanger. I close the door and change out of my clothes. Slipping into the dress carefully, I realize it fits like a glove. There's a slit that shows off my thick thighs, and I immediately know this is the dress I'm going to get. It's never this easy for me, but there's no weird lumps or ruffles in the dress. I look hot, so I walk out to show Ken.

"Hot damn! We're definitely getting that one." He moves his fingers, motioning for me to twirl for him, and I do. The dress spins with me, and I realize this one has pockets. Oh, fuck yes! I'm definitely getting this one just for the pockets alone.

"Ken! It has pockets!" He knows about every women's love of dresses with pockets.

"Well that settles it!" He laughs. "Go change and let's go."

I SHOW up to the event early, opting to get there before Barbie does so she can't kick me out or threaten to have security called on me. After picking my ticket up at the box office, I head to our table for the night. I'm feeling a mix of emotions, but I'm mostly eager to see Barbie again. I'm especially excited to surprise her. I don't know what Kelly's said to her, if anything, and that's a little unnerving, but I'm going for it. This is my chance to show Barbie how much I want to make this work between us.

I'm watching the door for her, and in the bundle of blue, red, and black dresses, I see a bright pink, strapless dress making its way into the place. Her back is to me, but I'd recognize that blonde hair anywhere. I stand, waiting for Barbie to see me.

Barbie steps into the room, and I'm immediately even more in love with her than I thought possible. She's wearing a pink, floor-length ball gown. The sweetheart cut shows off her cleavage beautifully, and the bottom—complete with bright pink tulle—flows effortlessly. She looks like one of those fancy Barbie dolls you get and want to keep in the box to savor their look. I could never get tired of looking at her, honestly. Her lips are painted a pink to match the dress, and her makeup is just subtle enough that you'd only notice it if you were *really* looking at her. She's glancing around the room, probably for her table, when she finally spots me.

We lock eyes from across the room, and for a moment it's like one of those rom-com moments where I forget anyone or anything else exists. Everything else is cancelled out as if I'm wearing those noise-cancelling headphones, but all my focus is on her. She's the only thing that matters. It only lasts a few seconds but it's long enough for a smile to form on my face. Just as quickly, her face falters, and I can tell she's less than thrilled to see me.

Barbie makes her way over to me and pulls me away from the table. "What are you doing here?"

"Nice to see you, too. You look lovely, by the way." I smile, ignoring her question.

"Kenzie, I'm serious." She stares me down.

"I might've gotten a call from your sister, and she might've told me to come and surprise you," I say sheepishly.

"I swear Kelly has no clue how to stay out of my business," she grumbles with an eye roll.

"I think she meant it to be a nice thing. She's rooting for us."

"It isn't her place to meddle in my life like this." Barbie groans.

"I think it's sweet. She cares about you so much." I smile.

Barbie stares at me like she isn't sure about what to do with me.

"Look, if it's really going to bother you, I can go. I don't want to force you to be around me if you don't want to."

Barbie hesitates, then sits down at our table and looks up at me. "Just sit down." She sighs.

"Okay." I laugh.

She avoids eye contact with me throughout dinner but finally glances at me during dessert, and I take the chance to start a conversation with her.

"So, how was work?"

"Are you really asking me about work? Was *how's the weather* too generic?" she teases.

"I was just curious how your day was."

"It ... it was complicated. Usually my sister is there to help but she's on vacation with my parents, and I had a little issue but I had to figure it out without her," she explains.

"Why aren't you on vacation with them?" I ask, confused. She's close with her family, so why isn't she with them?

"I have too much work to do. The company can't afford to have Kelly and I both go on vacation, especially at the same time."

"Life's too short to skip out on vacation, Doll Face." I wink.

She smiles and then looks away like she's affected by my wink. I like that I still have the chance to make her blush so easily.

"How was your day?" She's clearly changing the subject, but I let her. I don't want to push her too much too soon.

"It was okay. I had a shoot for a lingerie advertisement, and then Ken and I got Sushi. He's a doll, you'd love him," I say, realizing she's never met Ken.

"Is he just a friend or ...?" she asks, and I'm surprised she's even interested in knowing that.

"He's my very gay best friend. He's about as straight as I am." I laugh, knowing there isn't an ounce of me that would want to touch or go near a penis.

"Ah." She smiles and I can tell she's relieved.

"Don't worry, Barbie, I've only got eyes for one girl." I wink. Barbie blushes a bright pink to match her dress, and I know in this moment, I need to get my girl back. She's spent too much time not being mine, and I'm ready for her to be mine again.

After the charity ball, where we do very little dancing and mostly spending money donating to charity and bidding on things I don't remotely need, we head home. I insist on taking Barbie home, and for once, she doesn't refuse. We climb into the Uber, trying to gracefully slide in while wearing our fancy dresses, and we stop at her place first. I ask the man to wait, and I walk Barbie to the front door of her apartment complex.

"I had a really nice time tonight." I smile.

"I did too. Surprisingly."

"I'd like to see you again," I add.

"I-I don't know." She hesitates.

I take a step closer and erase the distance between us. I'm about to kiss her on the cheek to say goodnight when she closes her eyes and leans forward. Taking this as a sign, I step toward and press my lips to hers. It's a quick, chaste kiss that only lasts a few seconds, but it was just long enough to remind me what I'm pushing for. What I'm fighting for with her.

Chapter 6

Barbie

After the surprise Kelly pulled last night, I wasn't surprised to see Kenzie had texted me this morning. It's only nine a.m., and she's already texted me three times.

> Kenzie: Thinking about last night … 😊
>
> Kenzie: I want to see you again.
>
> Kenzie: We have a date tonight at six. I'll pick you up.

ONE PART of me wants to say no, but the other part remembers what it felt like to have Kenzie's lips on mine again. So, I text back a quick reply to let her know I'll be ready and then get back to my work. It isn't easy because I'm still thinking about Kenzie's lips and how she kisses me so effortlessly. I feel like I'm floating. Last night was so unexpected, but it was also one of the best nights out I've had in a long ass time. As much as I'm mad at Kelly for setting the whole thing up, it's also somewhat of a good thing. Not that I would ever admit that to her.

I head home after work and change into shorts and a pink blouse. I'm not sure where Kenzie is taking us but I hope it isn't anywhere too fancy. I have enough of that during the week with my job. I don't need to be wined and dined on a date. I enjoy more casual dates, so when Kenzie shows up on my doorstep wearing a jumper and a pair of sneakers, I'm relieved.

"Where are you taking me?" I ask her. She greets me with a kiss on my cheek, and I smile.

"It's a surprise. I had a photo shoot here earlier this week, and I thought you'd love this spot," she says as we walk toward the subway station. I'm surprised she knows how to use the subway system, but maybe she's relying on me to navigate.

"I'm using my app to get us there," she says, holding up her phone, and we board the subway toward Brooklyn.

"I can help if you tell me where we're going." I chuckle.

"Nope. It's my surprise for us." She's holding an oversized bag that is zippered shut so I can't see what's inside. The suspense is sort of killing me, but in a good way. I can't remember the last time someone put this much effort in with me.

We walk off the train and up a few flights of stairs. I'm looking around for clues but the only thing I can tell is that we're in Dumbo. Is she taking me to some touristy spot to see the Brooklyn Bridge? I frown. *Doesn't she know me better than that?*

Doll Face

"Don't worry. We're not doing something with lots of tourists, you'd hate that." She chuckles, reading my face.

"Oh." I purse my lips. I wish she would just tell me where we're heading.

"We're almost there." She leads me past the iconic spot where tons of people are trying to get photos of themselves with the bridges. Then she leads me past a garden looking thing and toward some rocks. We walk along the grass and she looks at me, puts up one finger gesturing for me to wait, and then starts unzipping her bag. She's like Mary *freaking* Poppins as she pulls out a big ass blanket, a picnic basket, and a bottle of champagne.

"Whoa," I whisper. The blanket is a bright pink, and I know she's done that for me. She lays the blanket down, sets up some of the food, and then motions for me to sit next to her.

"Here ya go." She hands me a plastic champagne flute and pops the bottle. She pours it all over us, then in the cup, and takes a hearty sip from the bottle. I'm not exactly sure why, but it turns me on.

"Cheers, to second chances." She winks at me, and I shake my head with a slight smile.

"I thought we could watch the sunset and just catch up," Kenzie explains.

I glance at the view ahead of us. There aren't too many people nearby, and the view is amazing. You can see the water and the Brooklyn Bridge without the brigade of people taking over. The city skyline rests behind it and off to the side, showcasing the pink and purples of the summer sunset.

"So, how was your day?" I ask with a stifled laugh.

"Not asking me about the weather?" she mocks.

"Hey, be happy I'm showing an interest in your job."

"Okay, my day was good. I did another lingerie ad but this time it was actually stuff I'd wear." She shrugs. I can't help it but now I'm picturing her in that lingerie set I saw on her Instagram, and I'm clenching my thighs together. Because fuck if I didn't think about getting myself off to that when I saw it.

"You okay? You look pale," she teases. "Something I said?"

"I don't know what you're talking about." I take a cracker off the plate she set up and force it in my mouth. I can't blush while I'm eating. Fuck my pale complexion for giving me up so easily.

"Have you been seeing anyone lately?"

"You mean besides you?" I joke.

"Yes." She clenches her jaw.

"No, I mean a few dates here or there but that's really it." I wait for her to say something but she just nods. "What about you?"

"I had one serious girlfriend, but she wasn't you. And I think she knew that I wouldn't be happy with her long-term, so she ended things," she explains. It hurts, but only for a second. She can have a life without me. She's only here for a week, anyway. Why would I care if she's seen someone in the five years that we've been apart?

"Oh," I mumble quietly.

"I think I've always been in love with you, Barbie." Kenzie smiles.

"I don't know how you could know something like that."

"What?"

"I don't know how you could be so sure of something like that," I clarify.

"It's just how I feel. I get if you don't feel the same

anymore, but you keep agreeing to see me so I think there's something here."

"I ... I ..." I don't know what to say so I follow my gut and lean in for a kiss. This time it's longer and steamier than our last. Our tongues tangle together, tasting of expensive bubbly and the crackers I've been munching on.

"I didn't see that coming," Kenzie says as I pull away.

"Neither did I."

"Oh, you have some of my lipstick on you." She leans forward with a napkin and brushes her fingers across my chin. She does it so slowly that we lock eyes, and I'm wondering what she's thinking.

I move my attention to the sunset in front of me, and I smile. It's beautiful. I take out my phone and snap a few photos of the sky before the sun sets completely.

"Do you want to go to our next spot?"

"There's more?" I ask, surprised.

"I rented a hotel room." She points to the building near us and at one of the windows with the view of the skyline. "It's right over there."

"Isn't that a little presumptuous?" I fold my arms over my chest.

"You're the one with your mind in the gutter. I did it so we could continue to watch the sunset without bugs biting you and maybe have some dinner ordered in since you hate going out," she explains, and I instantly feel like a jerk. She didn't pull that answer out of her ass; she had actually thought about it ahead of time.

"Oh."

"So, is that okay with you?" She smirks.

"Yes. That sounds nice," I add for good measure.

She starts to clean up the stuff around us, and I down the rest of the champagne in my flute before giving her the glass. She hands me the bottle to carry, folds up the blanket, and then we walk toward the hotel. It looks more like an apartment complex than a hotel. She heads right past the front desk to the elevators, and we stop on the third floor. After walking down a long corridor, she puts a key in the lock and I hear the clicking of the mechanism.

"Make yourself at home. I stopped by earlier after my shoot," she explains.

"Are you staying somewhere else for modeling?" I ask, confused.

"Yes, but I'm on a floor with all my model friends, and there isn't a view of anything."

"Ah." I nod.

"I really don't want you to think I'm just taking you here to try and sleep with you ..." She puts her hands on her waist. I gaze into her hazel eyes and take her hand in mine. I'm not sure why, but it just feels right.

Neither of us speak while I close the distance between us with a hand on her cheek, and she leans into it with a soft smile. I pull her face toward mine and kiss her lips with all the ferocity I'm feeling. Suddenly, I'm desperate for her. For more of her than I've had in so long. So I kiss her, letting her put her hands around my neck, mine around her waist, as our bodies press together.

"Is this what you want?" She pulls away, breathlessly, to ask.

"It is." I nod.

"Then come with me." She takes me by the hand and leads me to the closed blinds. She opens them with both hands and then looks back at me. I look at the bright pink sky and how beautiful her silhouette looks in front of it.

"Fuck, you're beautiful," I mumble.

"So are you," she says clearly.

She pulls me back in for a kiss against the windows. Her back presses against the glass, and we're suddenly frantic, pulling clothes off and lost in the moment. Her jumper comes off in one swoop. She tosses my T-shirt across the room, and I shrug out of my shorts. We're both in matching sets, mine pink and hers black, but we were clearly prepared for whatever might happen tonight. I giggle to myself, and she smiles, clearly thinking the same thing. As much as we said this wasn't going to happen, I think we both wanted it to.

"I think we should continue this in the bedroom," she whispers.

"Don't wanna give the neighbors a show?" I tease.

"Not for free." She winks and interlocks my hand in hers. She leads me to the bedroom down the hall, and we each unhook our bras as we walk. Once we reach the room, we climb into bed together.

Kenzie's body is just as beautiful as I remember it. Full of curves for me to kiss and love. She pulls me in for a greedy kiss while her hands start roaming my body. Her hands stop on my breasts, playing with my nipples, and I gasp into her mouth lightly. I reach for her breasts but she paws me away. She always loved being in control. I let her take over as she flips me on top of her and lies down on the bed.

"Sit on my face, Doll Face," she whispers with hooded eyes.

"A-are you sure?" I'm not exactly twenty-two anymore; we're grown adults. I honestly don't know if she can handle it.

"Sit on my face. Now," she commands, and I do as she says.

Hovering over her face, I lower my pussy over her

mouth, and she begins licking slowly. Then, without warning, she pulls me by the thighs and I collapse on her face, gripping the headboard. She begins working her tongue in a painstakingly perfect rhythm while I moan for her.

"Oh, Kenzie!" I call out, moaning and gasping while rocking my hips over her. I forgot how fucking good she feels. How well her tongue works my pussy.

She hums under me, and I feel the vibration shake me to my core. I play with my breasts, kneading them and pinching my nipples lightly as she sucks on my clit. I can feel my orgasm building, probably because it's been way too damn long since I've had sex—even by myself. My pink vibrator isn't used much anymore. I know I'm going to come hard and fast all over Kenzie's face. But if memory serves me correctly, she's going to love it.

"I'm so close!" I call out, and Kenzie doesn't let up.

Her tongue slides through my folds, she flattens it, and with a flick of it over my clit, I'm screaming a slew of curse words as I come for her.

"Oh my god! I'm coming!" I scream as I come all over her face, and she immediately laps my juices up.

When I finally steady myself, I climb off her face and lie in the bed next to her. She's covered in me, so she heads to the bathroom to grab a towel. When she comes back, she brings a warm washcloth to wipe me down, too. She spreads my thighs and rubs between my legs, cleaning me. It's a sentiment not lost on me. No one has ever taken care of me the way Kenzie has.

She pulls me in for a cuddle, and instead of fighting her, I lean into it. I just want to be as close to her as possible right now. Even though it's scary, and I could think of a million reasons why I shouldn't be intimate with her, I refuse to think of any of them right now. I melt into the possibility of us and all that we can be.

"It's too late, just spend the night with me?" Kenzie whispers in my ear. Even though I could argue it's barely nine p.m., I don't.

"Okay." I nod and let her hold me close.

Chapter 7

Barbie

The next morning, I wake up and look around the bedroom, but Kenzie is nowhere to be found. Surely she wouldn't leave. I throw a sheet around me and peek into the bathroom but it's empty. Then, I walk down the hall and realize the kitchen is empty, too. Her bag from last night is still here, which is promising. But where the hell could she have gone? I'm just about to start looking for my phone to call her when I hear the front door opening. Instead of doing anything rash, I pick up the nearest object—a wooden spoon—and the sheet I'm holding drops. Now I'm naked *and* defenseless to this intruder. I'm struggling to pick up my sheet when I throw the spoon at the person.

"Ow!" Kenzie groans.

"Oh, shit."

"What the hell are you doing?" Kenzie laughs at the sight of me. Completely naked, sheet on the floor, and a spoon between us.

"I thought you were a murderer!" I exclaim.

"And you were saving yourself with a wooden spoon?!" Kenzie starts laughing hysterically.

"It was the first thing I grabbed!"

"Well, anyway, I got bagels."

"That's where you went?" I ask. Duh, she wasn't leaving me alone. She was just out getting us food.

"Yeah, I thought we could have breakfast before you go to work."

"Oh, shit! Work! What time is it!?"

"It's just after seven a.m."

"I have an hour before I need to be there, and I have nothing to wear." I'm never this unprepared for work. This is going to be terrible. I can't go into my office wearing shorts and a T-shirt that I wore last night.

"I thought you might say that." Kenzie smiles and takes out her phone.

"What did you do?" I raise an eyebrow.

"I called your assistant when you fell asleep last night and asked her to grab you an outfit and meet you at the Starbucks that's a block away from your office. She'll be waiting for you. I knew you wouldn't want to stay in your clothes from yesterday, and it's too far to head home first," Kenzie explains.

"Really?" I ask. That was so fucking thoughtful and surprising of her.

"She'll be there at 8:45 a.m. with your outfit. She said she had to bribe your doorman but he let her into your apartment because she has the key." Kenzie shrugs.

"You really are amazing." I smile. Such a small gesture is going to make my day a million times better than I originally thought.

"Now, come have a bagel with me." A huge grin spreads across her face.

"I wish I could, but I really do have to go. I don't want to be late; I have an important meeting today." I head back into the bedroom to get dressed.

"Take one to go, then?"

"Yes, please."

"Good. I stopped by your favorite bagel place."

"How did you know my favorite bagel place?" I furrow my eyebrows together and look up at her as I slide on my shorts.

"I might have stalked your Instagram and found when you posted about them." She shrugs like it's not a thoughtful thing to do.

"Thank you." I smile.

"I'll butter one up for you and you can take it with you."

"Sounds perfect." I press my lips to hers, and I feel a warm sense of security when I do.

She smiles and heads to the kitchen while I look for my shirt. It's tossed aside, and I throw it on easily while I watch Kenzie in the kitchen. The idea of this being our life pops into my head. Could we really work? No, she's only here for a week, and last time we attempted long distance, it fizzled out right in front of us. I don't want to put myself through that again. I just need to enjoy this for what it is—a fling.

"Here you go, have a great day at work." She kisses my cheek, and I pull her in for a deeper kiss.

"Thank you." I blush, pulling away.

"No, uh, thank you. Can I see you for lunch today? I'm not taking no for an answer."

"I guess, yes then." I laugh.

I head out the door before she makes me commit to anything else, and I walk toward the subway. Thankfully, I always have my metro card on me, so I'm able to jump on the train back into the city. I meet Midge at the Starbucks closest to the office, that's not in the actual building so I wouldn't run into anyone. She's there waiting with my outfit and a change of shoes.

"Thank you! You're definitely getting a raise!" I promise her.

"Don't worry about it." She laughs.

I know she's my assistant but she might also be one of my closest friends.

I change and we both head to the office together. I have a big meeting with the company who designed the toys that turned into dildos. They aren't exactly happy about that, and I need to calm the company manager—a very expressive white man who is threatening to fire people he doesn't even have the authority to fire—down.

"I promise we're taking this very seriously. I have my whole team working on the next round of toys to be made right now," I assure him.

"You're just a child. I thought we had a meeting with the CEO of the company?" He scoffs.

"I *am* the CEO of the company. And I'd appreciate you treating me with as much respect as I'm giving you even though it's quite clear you're in this position because it's a family company. Unlike you, I earned my position here." I'm tired of men coming in and talking to me like this.

"I see." He sits down and looks over the papers I've given him. "I'll have you know my family company takes having me in charge very seriously."

"I'm sure they do. But my position wasn't just handed to me, and I deserve to be spoken to with respect," I say sharply.

"I'm sorry. I'd like to move forward."

"Of course, I'm happy to go over any concerns you may have moving forward." I nod.

"I want to see the new production line is running smoothly then."

"That we can do. I'll have my assistant escort you down, and we can meet again if any red flags are raised, but I'm sure that won't be necessary." I smile and head out of the office before he can say anything else. I'm not going to waste my time with an asshat like that.

I tell Midge to escort him down to production, and I head back to my office. It's almost time for lunch, and I still have a few more things to do before then. I leave a note on Midge's desk to not disturb me unless absolutely necessary. Just as I sit down to start working, I get a phone call from Kelly on the work line. I know it's her because I'm old, and she's one of the few phone numbers I actually have memorized for emergencies.

"Hello?" I didn't expect a call from her while she was on vacation.

"Hey, girlie!" she says excitedly. She's clearly been hitting the open bar at the resort.

"What's up, Kelly?"

"I was just wondering how the ball went," she says with an added giggle.

"It was okay." I don't give her any of the details she's so clearly searching for.

"Oh, no one unexpected showed up?"

"Like Kenzie? Yeah, she showed up."

"And!?"

"And what? I've told you countless times—stop meddling in my dating life. *Especially* with Kenzie. She doesn't need any help when it comes to thinking she has a chance with me."

"I'd say I'm sorry but I'm not. I want you to be happy,

and I've never seen you happier than when you were with Kenzie," she explains.

"Well, it might have worked out for the best."

"What!? Did something happen?"

"No, I'm not giving you any details, all you get to know is that maybe things aren't so bad when you meddle ... not that I want you to ever meddle again!"

"Yeah, yeah! All I'm hearing is that my plan worked well." She giggles.

"Anyway! How's the trip with Mom and Dad?"

"It's fun, I found this hot guy that I've been flirting with, and I've been taking advantage of the open bar." I know my sister all too well.

"Well, don't have too much fun and forget to come back home. Things aren't the same without you here," I tease.

"Oh, I won't. Unless the hottie asks me to stay, then who knows!" She jokes right back.

"Have fun and tell Mom and Dad the same. I gotta get back to work."

"Okay! Have fun! Tell Kenzie I say hello!"

I roll my eyes and hang up on her. I try to settle into the paperwork I have piling up on my desk. I'm not used to the extra workload I've taken on in Kelly's absence. Plus, I've been distracted, and my work is taking a hit. It's hard not to think about Kenzie when she's the only thing on my mind these days. I'm like a teenager all over again. I know this is more than puppy love, but still.

Each year, we host a fundraiser and donate the proceeds to Up, Up, Away's children's charity. I'm filing the paperwork when I think about inviting Kenzie. We had fun at the ball together, and I know I'd have more fun with her there on my arm. Last year I went on my own, and I was hit on by a variety of single men that didn't understand I'm only interested in women. I'm about to call Kenzie and ask if she wants a ticket when I realize the event is on the 30th of next month. She won't be here. My jaw clenches. She's only going to be here until the end of the week. Three more days and then she will back in London—where her life is.

I don't know what the hell I'm doing. Am I really risking my heart for a few days of fun? I'm too old for flings. Flings are acceptable when you're in your early twenties or going through a mid-life crisis—and neither describes my current status. I don't want Kenzie to be a fling anyway. I hate to admit it but I still love her, and I want her to be the real thing. *Does she feel the same?*

Ugh.

It's not like I can ask her to give up her job and move to the city to be with me. I certainly can't run Up, Up, Away from London. I need to be here to control the company; that's why I made the move from California all those years ago.

I'm overthinking this. I mean, I know Kenzie wants to be with me, but what the hell does that even look like to her? What does that mean to her? I should be asking her these questions but I can't bring myself to. I'm too afraid of her answers not matching mine. I just don't see any situation in which we could both keep our careers and be together. So what the hell are we doing?

Apparently setting ourselves up for disappointment and heartbreak when Kenzie goes back to London. And as much as I love her, I know I can't take that again.

Chapter 8

Kenzie

"Do you have any plans for the rest of the day?" Ken asks now that our only nighttime photo-shoot got canceled. Something about the photographer doing too much blow and ending up back in rehab. I don't care, it gives me more time to spend with Barbie.

"I'm supposed to meet Barbie for lunch," I say with a smile.

"I see." He eyes me up. "It seems like that's been going well. We haven't had much time to talk since you keep bailing the moment shoots are over," Ken teases.

"I only have a week to convince her that we should be together. I don't want to waste any time I have with her," I admit.

"And you're sure she's the one?" Ken asks, raising an eyebrow and looking at me with pursed lips.

"I know, you're unconvinced."

"I'm just realistic. I don't know if everyone has only one soulmate out there." He shrugs and looks in the mirror, fixing his blond hair.

"I've been in love before her, and I've been in love after her, but I've never felt this way about her or anyone else," I explain.

"Then I hope it works out for the two of you." He smiles. "I'm headed to the spa, I'll see you later." He blows me a kiss that I pretend to catch and we say our goodbyes.

I take my time getting ready for our big date. I know she'll be wearing her work outfit so I don't need to dress up too much. But I still like to look good for her. I settle on a pair of black slacks and a red blouse that shows off just enough cleavage to tease her. I'm about to curl my hair when I realize I'm running out of time. I want to get there just a little bit early, and I still have a phone call to make on the way.

I show up for lunch, not sure if Barbie will be able to leave yet. I know Midge said she usually takes her lunch at noon, but I want to make sure we have enough time to eat. She said she usually only takes an hour, and that isn't enough time to head to Casa Azul—one of our favorite places we used to go to in California. When I found out they had a franchise in New York, I knew we had to go. So, I called ahead, and our favorites are being cooked as we speak.

"She should be out in a minute." Midge smiles as I take a seat, waiting for Barbie to get off the phone. But when she does, she doesn't look happy to see me.

"You can come in," she instructs coldly.

"Hey, what's going on?" I raise an eyebrow.

"I don't think I should go to lunch with you," she says sharply.

"What? Why?" What the hell had happened from this morning to now?

"We're wrong for each other. We can't both get what we

want and have the careers we want. It's pointless to try this again when we both know how this ends."

"Whoa," I say aloud. I can't help it. It's like every fear she's feeling got highlighted in the last few hours.

"I just can't put myself through that all over again."

"I understand where your worries are coming from but I'm not asking for a lifelong commitment right now; I'm just asking you out to lunch."

"I know what lunch turns into."

"Dinner?" I joke.

"Kenzie." She frowns.

"I'm serious, Barbie. I know it's a lot but I'm only here for a week, so why can't we have this week and then go from there? I love you," I say quietly. I reach for her hand, and she lets me hold it.

"Well, I only have an hour for lunch," she says, changing the subject.

"I know. I'll make sure you're back in time." I grin.

"Promise?"

"Maybe with a minute to spare." I wink.

"Okay. I guess we can go to lunch."

"Okay." I take her hand. She's taller than me in her heels, and I love the way she confidently towers over me.

We head out of the building to the car I have waiting for us, and we dash across town to the restaurant. Her eyes widen when she sees the name of the place.

"Is this...?"

"Our favorite place from back in California. It's a chain, and it's the same owners, I checked."

"Thank you." She smiles. I know she isn't a fan of fancy restaurants but this is her only exception. I tell the hostess about our reservation, and she brings us to a booth in the back.

"Your food will be right out."

"We— did you order already?" Barbie looks at me confused.

"My girl only has an hour break. I had to be proactive. Hopefully your tastebuds haven't changed too much." I smile.

"You got the steak quesadillas with extra sour cream and the nachos we share?" Her eyes widen and I nod. I'm relieved to know her palette hasn't changed that much.

"Just for the record, we aren't wrong for each other," I say, repeating what she said earlier.

"I-I just...this is so much so soon," she admits.

"It's a lot but it doesn't have to be. If we're moving too fast, I can slow down, but I'm not going to hide how I'm feeling about you."

The food comes, interrupting our conversation. There's a few minutes of moans and groans from each of us about how good the food is. Then, I redirect the conversation to being about us when I know she's listening.

"I love you, Barbie. I need you to know that. I want this week to be something we can both remember for the rest of our lives."

"What if I want more than a week with you?" Barbie asks carefully.

"I-I don't know." Her face falls and I reach for her hand. "I'm not saying no, I just know how hard long distance was on both of us last time." She sighs.

"I know." She looks solemn. I wish I had more to offer her than a lousy *I don't know.*

"Second chances aren't real," she says like it's obvious.

"I don't believe that. I don't think I found you again for no reason," I admit.

"Second chances are for movies and books." She huffs.

We finish eating lunch, and I pay before we start heading back to her office. The car is waiting for us, and we're both quiet on the drive back to her office. I wish I had a better answer for her. Because more than anything, I want this to be our second chance at being together. I want this time to be the time it works out for us. I know I'm only here for a week but it isn't like I can't come back. She could visit me, too. We're just looking at it from all the wrong angles, and I need to show her that.

"Barbie, I'm telling you this could be our second chance because I believe we were made for each other. We're like Ken and Barbie—literally. We found each other in this life, and I never stopped thinking about you. I never stopped loving you, honestly. So I know it's a lot, and it's fast, but I also know how I feel about you, and I want to spend my life with you, however that may look." If she's going to end this, I need her to know all the facts about how I feel first.

"Kenzie." Her eyes are brimming with tears, and I pull her in for a hug.

"I love you," I whisper into her hair. Holding onto her tightly, I can't help but not want to let go. I'm afraid this might be the last time I hold her.

"I-I love you too," she whispers back. I pull back and look at her face. Her mascara is running, and her lipstick is smudged, but fuck if she isn't the most beautiful woman I've ever seen.

"You do?"

"God, of course I do," Barbie says, smiling.

"We're not wrong for each other, and I promise to prove that to you." I smile.

"Promise?" she asks.

"Promise." I nod. "Now, let's get you cleaned up so you can be a bad bitch at work." I smile. I take a napkin out of my purse and dry her tears. She fixes her smudged lipstick and wipes her face clean.

"I'll see you after work, just shoot me a text."

"Okay." She looks at her Apple watch. "You got me back here with a minute to spare. How did you do that?"

"I promised I would," I say with a mischievous wink.

With that, I turn to go but Barbie pulls me back in. She plants a kiss on my lips, and I feel an ease run through me. She smiles before walking in the building, and I feel better about leaving her. As much I want to ask her to skip work and spend the rest of the day with me, I don't want to get in the way of her job. I know she's trying to do the same for me, too.

Chapter 9

Barbie

5 years ago...

"Come on! We're not going to get into trouble!" Kenzie says with a squeal.

"Excuse me, but I know when you're lying!" I shake my head.

"You're already naked! You're more likely to get caught now," she points out.

It was her idea to sneak into our neighbor's pool and go skinny dipping. It's a way too hot California night, and our pool hasn't been cleaned from the party we threw last week. Covered in red cups and God knows what else, I wasn't daring to get in that cesspool. But then my adventurous girlfriend decided going skinny dipping was a good idea. Sometimes I wonder how much trouble she'd get into without me reining her in. But then again, how much fun would I get into without her?

"Come. On," she says again.

"Okay!" I squeal and jump in before I can think twice about it. I hit the warm water seconds later with it crashing *around us. It was warmer than I expected it to be. It was almost like jumping into an oversized hot tub.*

"Shit, I didn't think you'd do it." *She giggles.*

"Hey!" *I splash her and laugh.*

"Hey!" *She giggles again and splashes me back.*

"Why didn't you think I'd do it?" *I frown.*

"Because I didn't think you'd want to get caught naked by your grumpy neighbor."

"Eh, he'd be lucky to see us like this."

"Oh, I'm not worried. I've worn less for lingerie shoots." *Kenzie laughs.*

"Don't remind me." *I groan. I hate that I'm not the only one who gets to see her body, but I know I'm the only one getting it so* intimately.

"Oh, you like me bringing in the dough," *she teases.*

"I like you doing what you love. It's not like I need the money from your job," *I point out.*

"True. You should really let me contribute something to rent," *she complains again. It's a common occurrence. I don't mind paying for the place when I know she's struggling to pay bills on her modeling contract. They don't pay her half as much as they should.*

"You contribute earth shaking orgasms." *I bite down on my bottom lip.*

"Oh?" *She wiggles her eyebrows at me.*

"Yes, and you're the only one who can deliver those for me."

"Mmm," *she hums and swims over to me.*

My back presses against the cool wall of the pool, and our chests touch. She brushes my wet, blonde hair out of my eyes and places a hand on my face. I close my eyes, leaning into her. All my worries seem to fade away as she touches me. It's like she's taking them all out of my body with a simple touch. I feel at ease, and I almost forget where we are. It's just the two of us in this moment, and nothing else matters.

"I love you," she murmurs.

"I love you too," I say back.

It isn't the first time we've said it to each other. Both of us fell into the stereotypes of lesbians moving too fast. But what can we say? We both felt it, and four years later, we're still feeling it. It's terrifying, loving someone as much as I love Kenzie, but I trust her with my heart. I know she'll never do anything to hurt me. There's an ease about us.

"We should get married," she whispers kissing my neck.

"W-What?" I stutter. Did I hear her right?

"I love when you get that panicked look in your eyes. I said ... we should get married." She smiles and looks at me. I'm sure there's panic running all over my face. I can't help it. Is she being serious?

"Is this a proposal?" I ask worriedly. I don't want things to change between us yet.

"No. When I propose, you'll know it." She winks. "I'm just saying, is that something you'd want?"

"I-I think so," I admit. Maybe not yet, but it's something I've thought about casually, in passing.

"It's okay to say no."

"No, I want to get married; we're just so young," I point out. We're barely twenty-three and have our whole lives ahead of us.

"I just want even more time with you. We don't have to get married tomorrow, just know I'm thinking about it." Kenzie smiles.

"If I'm going to marry anyone, I want it to be you," I admit.

"Yeah?"

"I love you more than words can describe," I whisper. She presses her lips to mine, and I wrap my legs around her body. She holds onto me tightly and our bodies begin moving against each other's as we kiss. Our kisses deepen as her tongue swirls around my mouth and her hands roam my chest. She takes my nipple between her fingers and plays with my other breast, kneading it in her hand. I wrap my arms around her neck and pull her in close.

"WHAT THE HELL?!" A loud grumble comes from behind us.

"Oh, shit." My eyes widen and Kenzie uses her body to cover mine from his view.

"Get the hell out of my pool!" he screams.

"H-Hi, Mr. Ritcher," I whisper, not looking his way.

"B-Barbie?"

"Hi," I say again. I mean what else can I say? I'm completely naked in his pool. "I'm sorry for the disturbance, my pool is being cleaned, and we didn't think anyone was home. We can go if you can turn around."

"Oh. You're ... okay, right." He seems to shuffle away uncomfortably, and when I hear the door shut again, I jump out of the pool as quickly as I can, toss on my dress, and throw Kenzie her clothes. She's so busy laughing she can barely put her romper on.

"Kenzie! Get dressed! Let's go!" I scream.

"I'm coming!" She giggles and finally puts it on. We head through the gate back to our house, past the pool, and back inside our place.

"I TOLD YOU SOMETHING LIKE THAT WOULD HAPPEN!" I scream when we get inside. Kenzie is still laughing so hard she's crying, and I can't help but join her.

"It's not funny!" But I'm not very convincing while I'm cracking up with her.

"You didn't see the look on his face; he turned bright red when he realized we were naked." She laughs.

"Because it's embarrassing! I'll never be able to look him in the eye again!"

"Oh please, if anything he just got to see two hot women making out in his pool. He probably went inside to jack off." She shrugs as if it's nothing.

"Ew!" I squeal. I don't want to think of my neighbor doing that.

"It's natural, Barbie. I mean, we do it."

"Please do not equate us doing it to my burly neighbor doing it." I sigh.

"Okay, okay." She laughs.

"I'm going to take a shower, care to join me?" I ask, changing the subject.

"Yes, please." She smirks. But on the way to the shower, we end up on the couch, kissing.

Her hands are all over my body, and mine are all over hers. My lips press to her neck as she throws her head back in pleasure. I moan into her ear as she pulls up my dress and touches my pussy. I'm already soaked. I just want her to touch me.

"Please," I beg.

"Please, what?"

"Please fuck me," I moan out.

"Yes, princess." She smirks and slides her fingers inside me. She's pumping for a few minutes, and I can feel my orgasm building. But suddenly she's pulling her fingers out of me, and I groan in displeasure.

"I'll be right back." She licks her fingers clean and hops off the couch, heading for our bedroom.

She comes back a few minutes later with our pink strap-on and harness—and a big smile on her face. My eyes light up when I see it. Something about her putting it on and fucking me with it makes me go crazy for her.

"I want you bent over the couch, princess. Can you do that?" She smirks as she takes off her romper and straps up.

"Yes, baby." I bite down on my bottom lip in anticipation. Sliding off my dress slowly, I strip for her. She smiles as she looks over my body like it's her next meal. I walk over to the edge of the couch and kiss her first, feeling the strap-on hit me in the stomach turns me on even more than I thought possible. My arousal is dripping down my thighs.

"Bend over," she commands. I nod and bend over on the couch, sticking my ass in the air and leaning on my stomach. I feel her moving behind me. She touches me again, and I gasp out.

"Oh, fuck." I'm breathless as she pushes herself inside me.

"Mmm," she groans and puts a hand on my lower back to steady herself.

"Can you feel all of me, princess?" she murmurs.

"I can," I whimper.

"Touch yourself for me," she commands, and I glide my hand between my thighs, searching for my clit. Sliding through my folds, I wet my fingers before rubbing small circles around my clit.

"Mmm, just like that," she whispers. Kenzie grabs my ass with two hands and begins pumping, pushing her hips into mine with enough force to drive me wild. I can feel her hitting my G-spot each time, and my orgasm is building as I rub tight circles along my clit.

"I want you, baby," I call out.

"I want you to come for me, princess." She grabs a fistful

of my hair and pulls me back toward her. My ear is by her mouth, and I hear her gasp and moan with each thrust.

"*I'm so close,*" *I call out.*

"*Oh, baby—*"

MIDGE KNOCKS ON MY DOOR, and I'm quickly snapped out of my daydream. Is it still called a daydream if it's something that actually happened to you?

"Sorry to interrupt but there's a call for you on line three." She smiles.

"N-no worries." I don't mean to stutter but I can feel how red my cheeks are. I feel like I just got caught with my hand in the cookie jar. Thankfully, I wasn't doing anything I wasn't supposed to be—aside from fantasizing about my ex.

I pick up the phone but it's actually a call for Kelly so I take a message for her. I clench my thighs together and realize just how wet my panties are. I'm soaked from my little daydream, and it's all Kenzie's fault.

She's right. We were so perfect together before. Not just because of the amazing sex we had, but because of how she pushed me out of my boundaries and to be more myself. She pushed me to be happier, and even when it was crazy, like skinny dipping, I enjoyed the experience because it was with her.

We worked together before, and it's not like one of us cheated or hurt the other in some unforgivable way. We just grew apart when she moved to London. Things faded and I took over the toy company, which took up more of my time than I intended. While she was having modeling shoots all over the continent, keeping in touch became harder and harder. Maybe if we weren't so young things would've been different, but I try not to think about that now. I'm sure a lot of things could be factors—things I don't even realize.

Still, I have the chance to be with her now, and even if it is only for a week, I think it's worth it. It's going to hurt like a bitch when Kenzie leaves, but damn if it isn't worth it to be called hers for just a little while longer.

Chapter 10

Kenzie

I invite myself over to Barbie's apartment after work. I don't feel like going out again, and I'm pretty sure she doesn't either. We had an eventful and emotional lunch, and that's enough for one day.

I came prepared with a bottle of her favorite champagne, but in reality, I just want to lounge on the couch with her and maybe watch a shitty rom-com. Maybe we can watch *The Notebook* and she'll realize second chances do happen. Then again, that would further prove her theory that they only happen in movies and books. I sigh and knock on the door of her penthouse after being buzzed up.

Barbie opens the door, and I drop my jaw. She's wearing a bright pink bra that her tits are spilling out of, a tutu-looking skirt around her hips that covers what I think is a matching thong, and they're tied to garters with a pair of pink stilettos. I'm soaked just by the sight of her.

"Well, are you going to just stand there or are you going to pick up your jaw and come fuck me?" She smirks.

"Fuck, Barbie," I mumble. I groan as she walks away, and I get a view of her perfectly round ass in the thong.

"Come on, or I'll start without you." I almost fall to my knees at the thought. I enter quickly, put down the bottle of champagne, and follow her to the bedroom. I almost miss how pink her apartment is but then I catch it. There's not a speck of color that isn't her favorite. This place is entirely *Barbie*.

I get to the bedroom and she's already lying on the bed with her legs spread wide open for me. She's holding a toy to the outside of her thong and groaning lightly. *Fuck.* I think I just died and went to heaven judging by what I'm seeing.

"God, *Barbie*." I whimper. She makes me actually fall to my knees at the end of her bed, and I stare directly at her panty-covered core.

"I want you, Kenzie." She bites down on her bright pink lips, and I moan. I want to be the one to do that.

I start to undress—just the outer layers of my clothing. Tossing aside my shirt and shorts, I'm thankful I thought to wear my cute panties *just in case*. It's becoming abundantly clear that Barbie wants to make the most of this week together.

"I've been dying to taste you all damn day," I whisper in a growl.

"Then come have your meal." She spreads her legs even wider and tosses her toy aside. I'd have to use that on her later, but right now, I want to taste her.

Pushing aside her thong and sliding the tutu skirt up her thin waist, I begin slowly kissing her inner thighs. I leave wet kisses on her inner thighs, stopping to nibble just rough enough to tease her. My nose brushes against her core, and her hips buck against me. I smile, knowing how badly she wants this. I can see her arousal growing more and more with each second that I'm not fucking her. I press my flattened tongue against her core and moan at the taste of her. Always so fucking sweet—like my own personal brand of candy. I'm addicted to her.

"Oh, Kenzie," she moans my name lightly.

"Mmm," I hum against her core, and she lights up like a fireworks display.

"Yes!" she screams. Pressing my tongue to her clit, I lap up her juices.

"Kennnnzie," she groans out, and I've never heard anything sexier. I brush my tongue against her slit, sliding up and down her folds, trying to devour all of her.

"I need more." Barbie moans. I know what she's asking for but I don't want to give it to her yet. She wants my fingers inside of her. She wants to come. But I'm not done treating myself. I want to lick her pussy clean before I get there. So, I shake my head, and she moans, tossing her head back against the pillows.

"Not yet, princess, I want to savor you," I whisper against her.

"Kenzie, I need you."

I run a finger through her folds, just to tease her. "Oh, princess, I can tell how much you need me."

"Please," she begs with pouty pink lips.

"You look so pretty when you pout, princess." I smirk, running my fingers through her folds again, feeling her growing wetter and wetter in anticipation.

"Kenzie, please baby." She begs again and this time I give in. Something about her calling me *baby* really gets me going, probably the same way she loves being called princess.

"Who's my princess?" I ask as I slide inside two fingers to her core.

"M-me," she utters.

"And were you anyone else's princess while I was gone?" I curl my fingers inside her and begin to pump gently.

"N-No."

"Really?" I look at her and she nods, almost begging for more.

"R-really." She nods.

"Good girl," I say while thrusting my fingers harder inside of her. She gasps and almost flies up toward me. Her body is spasming as I begin fingering her harder, just the way she wants it. Just the way I know she likes it. She's moaning and gasping and pleading for more while I push my thumb against her clit and watch as she thrashes.

"I want you to be a good princess and come for me." I smile.

"Mmm, yes, baby." She moans and I clench my thighs together.

"I'm so close! Don't stop, I'm about to—" And instead of saying anything, she squirts liquid all over my hands and the bed as she moans my name.

"Oh, princess." I groan. It's sexy as hell watching her squirt just for me. I love making her come undone.

"Mmm." She hides her face in her hands, and I push them away, climbing next to her in bed.

"You never need to hide from me. You are so fucking sexy and incredible." I kiss her lips.

"Mmm, it's your turn, baby," she says against my lips. My eyes widen and before I can say anything, she's tugging down my panties and throwing them on the floor. Barbie dives between my thighs, and her tongue meets my clit almost instantly.

"Oh!" I gasp out. Her tongue feels like wet heaven as she licks through my folds. She presses her thumb against my clit, and my hips buck toward her face. Grabbing a handful of Barbie's hair, I push her face closer to my pussy and moan as she takes long, languid licks.

"Mmm, fuck me," I beg. The way her tongue moves and works against me is like something out of a porno. It feels too good to be true.

Barbie uses two fingers and thrusts them inside my core, and I let go of her hair as she reaches to paw at my chest. I unhook my bra, and she begins playing with my nipple, taking it between her fingers and pinching ever so gently.

"Fuck," I murmur. The only sounds you can hear are my gasps, Barbie's licks, and the sounds of the city traffic zooming past her building. But mostly, it's just us. I love the way Barbie feels against my skin, the way she's touching me, and how she hasn't forgotten exactly how my body works.

"Mmm, princess." I groan aloud and she speeds up, her tongue and hand working magic on my pussy. I can feel my orgasm building almost instantly.

"Fuuuck, I'm so close," I call out and she doesn't let up. One more flick of her tongue against my clit, and the thrust of her hand has me calling out her name loud enough for the neighbors to hear.

"Oh, fuck. Princess," I mumble as she comes up for air. I'm still seeing stars but I pull her against me for a kiss. I want to taste myself on her lips; something about doing that always drives me wild.

"I love the way you taste," she murmurs.

"You taste even better." I let my tongue swirl against hers and our tastes combine.

"Not possible." She shakes her head.

"Come here." I pull her into my arms and hold her close to my body. I can't see her face, but I hope she's smiling. I am, not just because of the orgasm I just had but because of the way she makes me feel.

"Can you stay tonight?" she whispers.

"I thought you'd never ask," I tease. She pulls the covers over us and moves her ass closer to my waist when I steady her. "You're going to make me want to touch you again."

"Is that so wrong?" she asks mischievously.

"Is that what you want?" I turn her toward me, and she's biting down on her bottom lip.

"I just want you."

"Then get over here." She faces me now, and her hands run down the sides of my body.

Barbie smiles, then leans in for a long, lingering kiss. Our tongues meet, her hands stop in my curls, and I run mine down her body. I pull her in close to me, gripping her ass, and she moans into my mouth. I want her body as close to mine as physically possible. I spent so long without her. I don't ever want to feel that again. Even just physically. I want to be as close to her in every sense.

"I need you." Suddenly there's a frenzy between us. We both feel it, we can't touch each other enough, our hands roaming faster and faster all around each other. I grab at her chest, and she reaches for my ass. I moan into her mouth, and she's sliding her hand to my core while I'm doing the same to hers.

"Touch me," she breathes into me.

"Yes, princess." I don't want to tease her, I just want to please her in any way I can. There's an intimate feeling about how we're touching each other. It's more than just sex, and I can feel her feelings through her fingertips and the way she's touching me.

My hand slips inside her, and I watch as her mouth opens. Her small gasps and moans match mine as she touches me in the same way. We each ride the other's hand, bucking and moving our hips in a frenzy. I want to come with her—want to feel her orgasm against my hand just as mine hits me. I want to feel her squirt all over me while my own orgasm flows through me. God, something about what we're doing is making me go wild.

"I'm so close," I choke out.

"Good, me too," Barbie says breathlessly.

"I want you to come with me." I whimper.

"Mmm," she moans out.

"Princess, be a good girl and come all over my hand for me." I moan into her mouth and she kisses me fiercely. Our lips barely meet as I see her orgasm building for her with the small O her mouth makes and the way she's throwing her head back. It gives me a heads up just seconds before her pussy explodes like Niagara Falls. Watching her come for me instantly causes my own orgasm to roll through me, and I'm screaming her name once again.

"Fuck!" we both say in unison, and then laugh. Lying against the pillows, we smile at each other. Something about our frenzy only made us feel closer. In this moment, no matter who sleeps in the wet spot, I feel happy to have Barbie back in my life. I can't imagine going back to having a life without her. It's fairly safe to say, I'm fucked when I have to board that plane two nights from now.

Chapter 11

Barbie

I run out of the office with tears forming in my eyes. The last thing I want to do is cry in or outside of work, but tears don't stop because you want them to. I immediately pick up my phone and call Kenzie. She's the only person I want to talk to right now.

"Hey, I'm so sorry. I'm on set, are you okay?" she asks in a hushed tone.

"Hi." I sniffle, I'm trying not to cry.

"Doll Face, what's wrong?"

"I had the worst day at work. Everything is going wrong, and I don't know what I'm going to do. I just want to see you," I admit.

"I'm so sorry. Do you want me to meet you somewhere later?"

"Or now?" I sob. There's a long pause while I cry.

"Hold on," she says, and I can hear some faint yelling.

"If you can't see me it's okay." I blow my nose and wipe my eyes.

"No, if you need me I'm there." She pauses again. "I-I have to—"

The line goes silent. I almost think she's hung up on me but the call is still going.

"Hello?" I say a few times but she doesn't respond. I wait a few minutes and almost think about hanging up, but I want to know what she was going to say.

"I'm on my way, Doll Face," she finally says. I breathe a sigh of relief and hail a cab to my apartment.

On the way, I cry in the back of the cab. I cry so hard the cab driver asks if I'm okay and if I need to stop anywhere but I insist he takes me home. We get to my apartment fifteen minutes later, and I'm grateful to see Kenzie standing outside with the doorman.

"Oh, Kenzie!" I run into her arms and she holds me tightly.

"Barbie, are you okay?" She holds my face in her hands and looks at me with panic in her eyes.

"Let's talk inside," I insist.

She leads me inside, and in the elevator, I collapse against her. I feel like all the stress of the day has hit me, *hard*. Kenzie doesn't speak and neither do I. I just need to feel her close to me. I'm not ready to say what's wrong yet, and I know she respects that.

"I love you," she murmurs into my hair and kisses the top of my head.

"I love you, too." We head into the penthouse and she holds my hand tightly.

"Do you want to talk about it?" she asks quietly.

"N-not yet," I admit. "Is that okay?"

"Of course." She nods. "Why don't I run you a bath and maybe after that we can talk about it? I need to get this makeup off me." She's wearing a ton more makeup than usual but that's probably from the shoot she was at. I don't ask how she left early—or maybe it was already over. I don't have the energy to think about it much right now. My mind is on replay from the day I had.

"Okay." She gets up and heads to the bathroom. I hear the bath water running. I start to strip down while she gets the bath ready. Suddenly, she's walking past me toward the kitchen, and I look at her, unsure what she's doing. I hear her looking for something but I don't ask what it is; I know she'll ask if she needs help.

I walk into the bathroom and step into the bathtub. She laid out a pink towel and a bath bomb for me. I'm about to ask her to come in and join me when she comes back. She's holding a glass of rosé and some roses she got me before our date.

"What are you doing with those?" I ask.

"I was thinking you could have a relaxing bath, just trust me," she says, and I nod. I sink into the hot water, and I'm instantly more relaxed than I was a few minutes ago.

Kenzie puts the pink bath bomb in the water, watching it explode, and then starts picking the rose petals off the roses and sprinkle them into the water with me. I'm smelling the scent of fresh roses, and I close my eyes, leaning into the water. All of the stress from the day seems to melt away, and I finally relax a bit. Just knowing Kenzie is there is enough to make me feel better.

"You are beautiful," she whispers.

"Thank you, Kenzie." I smile, not opening my eyes.

"I'm so fucking lucky," she murmurs.

"I'm the lucky one, you literally came running the moment I needed it," I say back. "That means so much more than you know," I say, looking at her.

She leans forward to press her lips to mine, and I relax even more.

"Here, have some wine." She hands me my glass, and I

take a small sip. It's delicious and exactly what I need right now.

"I thought we could order in some food, maybe something Thai or Indian? I know those are your favorites." She smiles.

"I would love that," I say with a groan.

"Is it okay if I go wash this makeup off in the shower?" she asks.

"Yes, there should be everything you need in there, and I can watch from here." I smile looking at the shower that's only a few feet away from the bathtub.

"Oh. that might be too distracting for you." She bites down on her bottom lip and winks.

"I hope it is."

Kenzie starts stripping out of her clothes, dropping her sweatshirt and sweatpants to the floor. A lingerie bodysuit remains, and my jaw drops. It highlights all of her curves, and her breasts are spilling out perfectly. I clench my thighs together in the water and groan at how beautiful and desirable my girlfriend is.

"Wow," I say aloud.

"Oh, this has to go back." She sighs.

"Well, you're going to buy one the second it becomes available because it's sexy as hell."

"Yes, ma'am." She laughs.

She takes the bodysuit off too, and hops in the shower. The water runs hot and begins steaming up the bathroom. It's enough to make me feel some type of way while looking at my delicious girlfriend in the shower. I don't know if it's for me but she parts her thighs and touches herself, giving me a show through the glass door. She stops to lather up her breasts and play with herself just a little. Just enough to tease me.

I slide a hand down my stomach and to my core, flicking my clit with a finger, just to relieve some of this ache. I can't tell how wet I am due to the bath, but fuck, I'm turned on. Then, Kenzie locks eyes with me and begins to moan. A light gasp escapes my lips, and I'm no longer lingering on my clit, I'm full-on touching myself now. I need a release that only she can provide.

"Don't be a tease!" I call out to Kenzie, and she laughs. Throwing her head back in the water, she looks like a supermodel. I know that's what she does, but fuck, to see her so natural and sexy does something to me. I pump two fingers in and out of my pussy. It's begging to be touched, and all I want is to come for her.

Kenzie opens the shower door, just enough so I can see her run her hands down her stomach and to her pussy. She parts herself open and begins playing with her swollen clit. She's enjoying this just as much as I am. This is exactly the release I need after the day I had.

"I want you to moan for me, princess," she commands, and I do. Pumping my hand even harder against myself, I gasp and moan for her.

"Oh, fuck!" I call out and brush my thumb over my swollen sex. I'm so close and I *need* this.

"You can do it, princess. Come for me." She's playing with herself while water and soap drips from her wet body. She's a fucking sight to see.

"Oh, Kenzie," I call out one last time, and I'm seeing stars. I feel a release, and I'm thrashing in the water, losing all control of my legs as the orgasm rushes through me.

"Fuck." I peel my eyes open to see Kenzie coming from her own orgasm—which is equally as sexy. I push the stopper for the tub and rise, deciding to join her in the shower to rinse off. But in all honesty, I just want to touch her.

Our lips meet, crashing into each other's, and we're struggling to pull apart. That is, until the water runs cold. Then we both rinse, dry off with fluffy towels, and head for my room. We both climb into bed—naked—and cuddle under the covers.

I pull out my brush from my nightstand, and Kenzie takes it from me. I thought she was going to borrow it and brush her own hair. Without saying a word, she begins running it through my blonde locks. It feels magical and intimate; I've never had someone I love brush my hair for me—aside from my mother. But this is different. Kenzie doesn't have to. She *wants* to.

"I love the way that feels." I sigh, leaning into her.

"I love you." She tilts forward and presses her lips to my shoulder.

"I love you too." I smile. "Let's order some food."

"Okay. Let me grab my phone." She stands and heads for her bag that's across the room. Picking up her phone, she sighs and then starts typing.

"What do you want, Barbie?" I rattle off my usual order and tell her the name of the place nearby, then she calls in an order for us.

Twenty minutes later, we're deep in butter chicken and naan in my bed. I'm putting on some shitty rom-com that neither of us are really paying attention to while we eat. I know she's patiently waiting to ask me about what happened at work today, so I wait until we finish our dinner and then sigh. Kenzie's phone rings a few times until she finally puts it on vibrate, insisting she doesn't need to pick it up.

"Ready to talk about it?" she asks.

"I guess."

"You don't have to, but I think you'd feel better if you do."

"The board is attempting to buy me out of the company." Kenzie's phone buzzes on the nightstand, and she ignores it again.

"What does that even mean?"

"So, there's a board that runs the company. Technically, they are under me, but with a majority vote of something they could outrank me. It's rare but they've been trying to outbid me for years now. Then today they found out about the dildo fiasco because one of the men on their board went to his dad and complained about me. He's a douche and I told him off so I'm sure it was personal. But the mess up happened under my control, and now they're saying I'm unfit for my position. Not to mention they don't like the fact that I'm a single *woman* running the company—a single woman who wears nothing but *pink*. They don't take me seriously even though I bring in the revenue," I explain.

"Jesus, so you just got hit from all angles then?" she asks.

"I did. Plus I found out my assistant, Midge, is pregnant, so in a few months I might be losing her, too." I sigh.

"I'm sorry, Barbie. What are you going to do?"

"Well, there isn't much I can do besides show the board they're making a mistake or ask my parents step in on my behalf, but I'd prefer to handle this on my own. It just sucks it happened while Kelly is on vacation."

"I understand. I'm really sorry this happened to you," Kenzie says.

"It's okay. Thank you for being here for me. It means a

lot that you were able to come over." I kiss her lips lightly. I don't know what I would've done if I couldn't see her tonight. It was like I knew I could handle it on my own. She makes everything better just by being here with me.

Chapter 12

Barbie

I'm sleeping soundly when I hear a phone ringing. At first, I think it's part of my dream, but the more it rings, I realize it's real life. It's probably someone from work calling me. Although, it's a Saturday, and they know not to contact me on the weekend unless it's an emergency. Besides, my phone is usually kept on vibrate. I reach for the nightstand and realize it's Kenzie's phone. Didn't she put that thing on vibrate last night? I hear the shower running so I check the caller ID—*Manager Carla*. I don't want Kenzie to miss anything important, and judging by how many times they've called, I should probably pick up.

"Hello?" I yawn.

"Kenzie?" Carla says.

"No it's Barbie, her ... uh ... girlfriend." The word feels unfamiliar on my tongue, but it also feels right.

"Oh, Barbie. The family emergency." She scoffs.

"Excuse me?" I ask, confused.

"You do know you're the reason Kenzie walked off set yesterday in the middle of a shoot, right?" she snaps.

"I—"

"If she ever wants to work with this agency again she needs to give me a call back right away. What she did yesterday was not only disgraceful but also a breach of her contract," she says, her tone full of bite.

"I-I'll tell her to give you a call back." I hang up before she can yell at me again.

I sit there looking at the phone in my hands and sigh. *I* was the reason she left her photoshoot? I don't want that sort of responsibility. Why didn't she just say she couldn't come over? I know I was crying, but fuck. This feels like a weight of pressure on my shoulders that I don't need right now. I quickly hop out of bed and start running around the room looking for clothes. I toss on the closest pair of shorts and a tank top, grab my sneakers, and head out the front door. I don't know where I'm going, but I had to get out of there.

I know it's lame, leaving her behind, but I'll go back ... *eventually*. I just need some time to think about everything. Or maybe some space to think about what was right for both of us. I'm not leaving her or breaking up with her, I think I need some space. I'd rather not find said space in the New York City subways, but I left her in my apartment, and I don't have much of a choice. I decide to hop on the nearest subway and ride until the last stop. Then, I get back on in the opposite direction, just happy to be going *somewhere*.

It's already been over an hour; she's probably out of my apartment already, right? I mean it isn't like she's camping out in someone else's place all day, is she? No, she probably got out of the shower, didn't find me, and then went on her way. I turned my phone off so I don't know if she's calling or texting me. I don't want to know.

"Change, miss?" a homeless man asks, jingling a cup in front of me. I ignore him; I don't have any cash on me, and

I'm not trying to get hurt on the subway. "Bitch," he mutters and keeps walking.

I sigh. It isn't enough to be having the two worst days possible. Now I have to deal with some stranger calling me a bitch on the train. I let it go and try to think about Kenzie. It's just a lot to feel like she put her career on hold for me. Even just for a day. And what about when she leaves tomorrow? Is she going to come back? Will we try long distance again? I feel like there are too many possibilities, and I can't just breathe.

I think about work today and I know it seems stupid. I know it does, I'm in my twenties and I didn't have days where I cried for no reason. But between the board and Midge telling me she was pregnant, it felt like a lot. Maybe I'm hormonal or something because all of a sudden it felt like all these things combined just sent me over the edge.

Midge telling me she was pregnant was about thirty seconds of being happy for her and then panic and fear set in. She was younger than me and she was about to have her life all figured out with someone she loved. She didn't have a girlfriend who lived across another continent and didn't know if things would work out between them. I felt jealous and stressed and yeah, it was one of those days where I made it all about me. To Midge, she'd never seen anyone happier for her but inside it was frustrating as hell. Probably the thing that broke the camel's back or whatever the saying is. I just wished it was me who had their life and their partner figured out like that already.

I know who to talk to. I turn my phone back on and ignore all of the messages and missed calls I have. I click on my favorites and call Kelly. She'll know exactly what to do. I get off the subway at a random stop and decide to walk. I don't have a direction, I just need somewhere I can talk with service.

"Hey sissy, what's up?" Kelly's sipping on something; I can hear air in an empty straw in the background.

"I your advice." I pause. "And I need you not to gloat about it."

"No promises." She laughs.

"Kelly," I groan.

"Okay, okay. No gloating." I can picture her nodding for me.

So, I explain the whole situation from start to finish without leaving out any details. If she's going to give me honest and unbiased advice, then she needs all the details for once.

"I'm just anxious about what it means for us and if there really can be an us," I explain.

"Barbie, you're telling me that the girl you love called off a very important shoot to her. She ran to your side, bringing all your favorites, and spent the night with you to make sure you're okay. But you aren't sure what that means? Are you stupid?"

"What?" I laugh. "I don't think so."

"Is your brain made of plastic?"

"No." I roll my eyes.

"Then go be with your fucking girl! She loves you and yes it's scary but it doesn't have to be as long as you have each other. You're both older now and know what you're doing and what you want. So talk to her and be clear and see if she can meet your needs. But I'm pretty positive she can."

"Really?"

"I swear sometimes I think you can't see the whole picture." Kelly laughs.

"I just don't want to get hurt again."

"I know, and I can't promise that won't happen. But at least you can try. You're protecting your heart, but you don't want to put up so many walls that no one can get in."

"You're right." I nod even though she can't see it.

"Just go find your girl and be with her already. This is too many years in the making, and you told me I can't meddle anymore."

"Okay." We say our goodbyes and I sigh, looking up at the street signs. Subconsciously, I'm already heading toward home. I continue down the avenue, walking a normal pace. Then it starts raining. I take it as a sign, so instead of getting on the subway, I walk in the rain. It's a warm summer rain that feels like a drizzle instead of a pelting. It takes a while, but while I'm walking the drizzle turns into a lighter rain, and my clothes get wetter.

I need to get home, change, and find Kenzie. With fresh clothes and a new sense of things, I will feel a ton better than I did this morning. I know no matter what, Kenzie and I will be able to work things out. I just have to give her a chance to talk about everything.

When I walk into my apartment building, I'm confused when I hear shuffling as I stand outside my door…

Chapter 13

Kenzie

I wish Barbie would join me in the shower, but I want to give her a little bit more sleep since she had such a stressful day yesterday. So, I take my time in the shower and wash my hair thoroughly, scrubbing my skin clean before wrapping a warm towel around my waist. Of course it's pink and fluffy because I'm still at Barbie's apartment. I pad into the bedroom and look for my clothes. I'd have to settle for wearing last night's outfit since I didn't think to bring a change of clothes.

I turn around to wake up Barbie when I realize she's not in her bed. I look around the empty room, confused. Where could she have gone? I thought maybe she was doing what I did and went to get breakfast ... but wouldn't she have left a note? Or come to tell me? I'm about to call her when I realize my phone isn't on her nightstand anymore, it's in the middle of the bed. I look at the call log. I have missed calls from Ken, my agent, and my manager, but the last call lasted for several minutes, which can only mean one thing: she talked to my manager. I don't care that she picked up my phone but I can only imagine what my manager said to her. *Fuck.*

I think back to the shoot yesterday.

I'm sitting on the set of a lingerie shoot waiting for it to start. I hate when these things run late; it's like they have zero regard for how we're people who need to do things—like use the bathroom and eat. It's already been an extra two hours of waiting because of shit like the photographer showing up too high to function and the lighting being "too bright" for him. I thought he was joking at first but then he insisted someone find him a pair of sunglasses. It took longer than you'd think in the summer in New York City. Apparently he wanted a certain brand, and I'm having less than good faith about how these pictures are going to turn out.

"Perk up, we can probably go out after this," Ken says, smiling.

"If this shoot is ever over." I groan. I look in the mirror at the pounds of makeup layered on my face and sigh. Is this still what I want to do? Lately it feels like more of a chore compared to wanting to spend time with Barbie. But then again, that has less to do with my job and more to do with wanting to spend time with Barbie.

"Okay, models!" the photographer finally says while wearing his new Ray Bans.

"I want you, you, and you on set." He points to me, Ken, and Daisy. We are all quiet as we wait for further instructions, like poses, the theme of the shoot, or any other information for us to do our job, but it doesn't come.

"Well, don't just stand there. Pose!" he shouts, looking at us like we're morons. I hate when photographers act like they're the ones in charge just because they make a little bit

more money than us. Finally, the director of the shoot gets up from their chair and saunters over.

"I need magic. Pretend you're about to all make love."

It's not the first time Ken and I have been pushed together as lovers. We get it; we'd make some hot ass babies. He's already offered to be a sperm donor and cool uncle Ken if the time ever came. With Daisy, it's a new dynamic, so we make sure to include her. She's beautiful with long red hair and curves, like mine, for days. She's also really brilliant, the only one of us to actually go to college before being scouted.

"Yes!" The photographer is happy now, dancing around the set. Until he jumps too high and then complains of a headache. So we're all told to have a seat and take another break.

I sit at my station and pull out my phone. I want to send Barbie a quick text when I realize I've missed three of her calls. Something must be wrong. I call her back instantly, even though phones on set are kind of a no no.

"Hey, I'm so sorry. I'm on set, are you okay?"

"Hi." Barbie sniffles. She's crying.

"Doll Face, what's wrong?" I ask quietly, using her special nickname.

"I had the worst day at work. Everything is going wrong, and I don't know what I'm going to do. I just want to see you."

"I'm so sorry. Do you want me to meet you somewhere later?"

"Or now?" She sobs.

I hesitate. I can't leave in the middle of a shoot, but in all the years I've known Barbie, she's never cried over something small. If something is happening to make her sob and ask to see me, I know it must be big.

"Hold on," I tell Barbie and try to think of something.

"Okay! Models back on set," the director yells. Fuck.

"If you can't see me it's okay." I hear her blowing her nose.

"No, if you need me I'm there," I say even though I don't know what to do. I've never had to choose between Barbie and my job before.

"Models!" the director calls again, and I realize everyone's waiting on me.

"I-I have to—" I'm about to say I have to go when the director comes up to me. I quickly put Barbie on mute so she can't hear anything for a second and put the phone down.

"Excuse me? Model? I know you're not hard of hearing since you're on the phone but it's time to get back on shoot," he snaps.

"I'm sorry but this is a family emergency."

"That's a hoot, you don't have any family. We are your family." My manager, Carla, scowls. That was a low blow, and she knows it. Sure, I'm not in contact with my parents but that isn't something I want to have thrown in my face.

"It's a family emergency, and I have to go," I say, and I start collecting my things.

"If you leave, you're jeopardizing your career," Carla says, grabbing my arm.

"It's an emergency," I repeat. It's like they aren't hearing me. I've never done something like this before and they know it. I'm not like some of the girls who break a nail or get their period and can't work. I'm always on time and ready. So to not be able to cut me a little leeway when I have an emergency feels like a slap in the face.

"I need to go." I grab my phone, toss on a pair of sweatpants and a sweatshirt, and leave the shoot.

I unmute Barbie. She's still crying when I pick up.

. . .

"I'M ON MY WAY, Doll Face, don't you worry about a thing," I tell her.

INSTEAD OF GUESSING what she said, I call Carla back to find out exactly what she said to Barbie. Once she answers, I know I'm in for an earful.

"Oh! There you are. Sending your girlfriend to answer your phone first was a slick move. I gave her an earful already," she snaps.

"I wasn't sending her. She didn't know about yesterday."

"She didn't know she was the reason you left a very important shoot for nonsense?"

"It wasn't nonsense and I don't have to explain my personal life to you," I snap back.

"Well, with that attitude you might not have a professional life either."

"Look, I'm sorry I left the shoot but it was a family emergency, and in all my years with the agency, I never once left or even arrived late. So, you might want to cut me some slack. I'm one of the longest models you've had, and I deserve an inch of respect and some flexibility," I explain. "Now, what did you say to my girlfriend?"

"I basically told her she was the reason you were in trouble with the agency and that it was some bogus emergency," she says.

"Well, that wasn't your place. She has enough going on without you putting things on her that aren't her fault." I growl.

"Are you coming to the shoot tomorrow?" she asks angrily.

"Yes. Like I said, I've never been late or missed one. I'm

not starting now." I hang up before she can say anything else.

I pace around the room, looking for a sign or something. If I go after her, I might not find her, and then there's no way she'd let me back in so we can talk. I know how stubborn she can be. But if I stay here will she come back? I mean, it is her home so she *eventually* has to come back. But will she be upset with me for not coming after her? I hate this. I just want to go back to last night where we were sleeping together, and I was thinking about forever with her.

Just as I'm pacing around the room, an idea hits me. I pick up my phone and call Ken. Thankfully, he picks up on the second ring. I know we don't have any shoots today so he's free as a bird and owes me a favor. Once I tell him the plan, he agrees and he's at Barbie's apartment within the hour.

"Thank you!" I kiss him on the cheek and take the bag from him. I owe him for this.

"Of course. I can't stand in the way of true love. Besides, Carla is way out of line. You had to put your love first; I've never seen you do that so she must be something special."

"She really is."

"Well, I'll get out of here before she comes back. Good luck!" He hugs me and is out the door and into the elevator in a matter of a minute or two.

I wait in Barbie's apartment for her to show up, knowing I might be kicked out the second she arrives. No matter what, it'll all work out. She just needs some time and space to cool off—to think about things. I get that, but I need to show and prove to her that I'm not going anywhere. I hear the ding of the elevator and the key at the front door, and not long later, Barbie's walking in.

"W-what are you still doing here?" She looks at me,

with rounded eyes and raised eyebrows. Her clothes are soaked as if she walked through the rain but I don't ask about that.

"I thought we could talk." I smile.

"There's nothing to talk about. I talked enough with your manager," she snarls.

"Barbie, you didn't get the full story."

"Then tell me you didn't leave work for me. Tell me you didn't almost get fired because of me." She crosses her arms, and I stay silent.

"See!" She lets out a sigh.

"Barbie, of course I chose you over work. I'm not saying I always can or it'll be easy to. But I chose you because you *needed* me. And I would do it again in a heartbeat." I huff.

"But that's a lot of pressure to put on someone."

"So don't put that pressure on yourself. There was a reason I didn't tell you about the shoot," I explain.

"So you waited here all day?" she asks.

"I did." I nod. "I had Ken stop by with supplies I thought I might need to smooth things over."

"What kind of things?" She eyes the bag curiously.

"Roses, your favorite. Your favorite kind of champagne and a box of your favorite chocolates—which are very hard to find." I laugh, pulling the things out of the bag one by one.

"But what are we doing? You have to leave tomorrow," she says.

I knew this would come up today. We've been avoiding it all week.

"I've already decided I'm quitting my job in London. I can be a model anywhere but I can't have you if I'm in London."

"Kenzie, you can't just give up your job and move

halfway across the world for me. I mean, what if it doesn't work out?"

"Barbie, I know you're scared, and that's okay. But I keep telling you I'm not going anywhere. I've left you before, and I can't do it again. I've never stopped loving you, and I want the chance to be with you and get to show you that. I love you more than words can explain," I say, smiling.

Barbie has tears forming in her eyes. "Promise me you'll be a model here? That we can find a New York agency and you'll still follow your dreams? I never want to stand in the way of your career or your dreams. I love you so much that I want you to be able to have both."

"Okay. I'm sure I'll find something eventually." I nod. Why hadn't I thought about switching agencies? I'm sure it's much easier than either of us have thought.

"So, you're staying?"

"Well, I have to go home and get my things and close out my apartment, but I'll be back as soon as that's done, and then yes. I'll be here permanently. With you, Doll Face." I wink.

"Then we better make the most of tonight."

Before I can say anything else, Barbie is pressing her lips to mine.

Chapter 14

Barbie

I lead Kenzie into the bedroom with our hands intertwined. If this is our last night together for a while I want to make the most of it. I want to spend every second we have wrapped in her arms and tangled with her tongue.

"I want you," I whisper against her lips.

"I want you too." She smiles, her eyes darkened with desire.

An idea pops into my head. "Get in the bed. I'll be right back." I wink.

Before she can reply, I run to the kitchen, grab two glasses, the bottle of bubbly, and my tray of ice cubes—which just so happens to be shaped like hearts. Kenzie is lying in the silk pink sheets, already naked and waiting for me. Her body is on display, and I clench my thighs together and bite my lip at the sight of her. Fuck. She is so damn sexy.

"Ooo, what's that for?" She smirks.

"I want to drink it out of your belly button." I wink.

"Fuck yes." She nods.

I place the glasses on my nightstand, pop open the bubbly, and take a large swig in my mouth. I pour the rest in the cups and pop two ice cubes in the glasses. I toss off all my clothes, except my thong, and then I lean over the bed, holding the bottle as I start kissing Kenzie.

I start at her lips, peppering quick kisses along her jawline, down her chest. Stopping at each of her breasts, I watch her nipples pebble, and then I move down her stomach. I kiss her stretch marks and around her belly button before pouring just a dash of champagne on her.

She giggles at how chilly it is as I bend down to slurp it out of her bellybutton, letting my tongue linger on her.

"W-What if we used the ice?" Kenzie asks looking at the ice cubes next to her.

"You want to?" I smirk.

"Yes." She nods.

I put the bottle down and reach for the ice cube tray. I place a small piece of heart-shaped ice into her mouth for a second before pulling it out with my tongue. She helps pass it into my mouth, and the cool sensation only heightens my arousal. We kiss, passing it back and forth a few times as it starts to melt.

I reach for her chest, straddling her on the bed as we let the ice melt in our mouths. Now that my mouth is nice and cool, I lean forward to suck on her nipples, letting my cold tongue swipe over each pink, pebbled nipple. She moans under me, and I know it must be an overwhelming sensation. So I take the last bit of the ice out of my mouth, and squeeze it in my hands, pouring the ice water down my chest and locking eyes with Kenzie as my own nipples harden. Two rosy buds pop in the air as the cold water hits them.

"Fuck, princess," she moans out. She reaches for my

breasts and her soft hands touching them paired with the cold ice water feels like heaven. She reaches toward the nightstand for another piece of ice; this time she's in charge.

Kenzie runs the ice on my breasts, around my nipples, and down my stomach. I gasp out each time the ice hits a new, sensitive area, my arousal building quickly.

"Oh princess, I love the way you perk up when I touch you," she murmurs.

"Don't tease me," I beg. I'm sitting on her lap in just a small thong as an increasingly wet patch grows on the fabric.

"Oh, but I love it when you beg," she says, desire coating her voice.

She runs the ice cube down my stomach and stops at my core. "Oh!" I gasp, feeling the cool sensation take over my body. The warm, wet center of my core melts the ice almost instantly, but not before leaving behind an equally cool sensation.

"Oh, baby," I moan for her.

She picks up her glass of bubbly and pours some in her mouth. Then, she surprises me by leaning forward and pouring it into my mouth. It should be gross, the act alone, but something about the way she does it only turns me on even more. She could probably do anything, and I would find it sexy.

"Mmm," I murmur against her lips. She bites down on my bottom lip and pulls it out, just far enough, then sucks on it gently.

I push her shoulders back into the cool satin sheets. Grabbing one last ice cube, I pop it into my mouth. Diving between her thighs, I push her legs wide open and lick her clit slowly. She moans, clenching my head between her thighs under my touch. I don't know if it's because of the ice or my tongue alone, but she is dripping wet and extra sweet today.

"God, I love you." She whimpers and her hips buck against my face, drenching my chin in her juices. I continue licking and sucking on her clit, taking in all of her. The ice begins melting in my mouth, giving me easier control over it as I run it up and down her slit. Her swollen sex is throbbing from the ice.

"Oh! I'm close," she calls out as I slide a finger up to her clit. She continues whimpering, and as the ice melts, I keep my tongue on her clit and slide two fingers inside her. Pumping and curling my fingers, I rock them into her center. I feel her core tightening against my fingers as she's coming. Her back arches off the bed, and I hear a plethora of curses as she orgasms around my hand.

"Oh, fuck, princess." Kenzie pulls my face into hers instantly and pushes me back into the bed. My head hits the pillows as she's climbing on top of me. Without missing a beat, her thigh is between mine, and we're scissoring.

"Oh, god, yes!" I moan. I want to close my eyes and enjoy every second of this, but instead I keep them open and glued to Kenzie. She does the same, her hazel stare boring into mine as we rock together.

"Yes!" I scream as our wet pussies glide across each other's.

"I want you to be a good princess and squirt all over me," she commands. I bite down on my bottom lip and hold back a moan but she takes my face in her hand and looks at me. "Don't hold back, I want to hear every last whimper out of you."

"I love you!" I call out breathlessly. I'm trying to hold back on purpose, but fuck if it isn't the hottest thing for her to want my sounds.

"I love this. Being with you, I love you. So give me all of you, Barbie," she says quietly.

"I love you too, God. I don't ever want to be with anyone else." I whimper as our bodies move together as one.

Kenzie nods but moans as our clits rub together. My hands reach for her breasts that are hanging in my face, and I position one so I can suck on her nipple and watch as she moves her hips enough for the both of us. One hand on my thigh, the other on my left breast, she rocks back and forth, causing the friction that drives me wild. Something about this position makes it my favorite, and she knows that. It's intimate and sexy as hell.

She rocks and I gasp out for her. "I'm so close!" I say.

"Be a good girl and come for me, princess," she says, glaring into my eyes.

"Yes! Yes! Yes!" Our hips rock together, and my orgasm flashes though me. I feel it in my clit, and my pussy gushes a waterfall between us. The overflow pushes Kenzie into her second orgasm, and her mouth forms a wide O as she comes for me again.

"Oh, fuck," I mutter.

"God, you're so sexy." She presses her lips to mine, and we roll around the bed, both of us fighting to be on top. Neither of us wants to stop, and honestly, why do we need to?

"Get my toy out of my drawer," I command.

"Yes, ma'am." She winks, grabs it, and goes to hand it to me.

I shake my head and she looks at me, with furrowed brows. "I want you to use it," I whisper.

"On me?" Her eyes widen when I nod.

"I want you to practice touching yourself for an audience. If we're going to make long-distance work, even just for a few weeks, we're going to need some sexy FaceTime sessions," I explain.

"Ah, I like the way you think." She smiles and sucks on her bottom lip. She takes the toy, turns the speed on low, and presses it to her clit. With a low buzzing, she draws small circles around her.

"I want to see you touch yourself too," she commands.

"With pleasure." I nod. I'm no stranger to self-pleasure, even if there's an audience this time. I want my girl to see exactly how fun it can be.

I reach my hand between my thighs and start to flick my clit gently, playing with the sensitive bud while I look at Kenzie. I don't have the best view, so I move to where I can see between her thighs. The pink toy bounces in and out of her pussy. The device has more of her juices on it each time it peeks out. I'm already on edge from our sex; I barely need to warm myself up. I'll be coming again in mere minutes.

"Fuck, I love the way you touch yourself." I pant.

"Mmm, me too." She tosses her head back, and the toy disappears deeper into her wet pussy. "I love your body."

"Oh, princess," she calls out, closing her eyes. I slide a finger in my pussy, mimicking her motions, and the moan that leaves my lips has her pumping the toy even faster.

"You look so beautiful moaning my name baby," I whimper out.

"I'm so fucking close, princess. Moan for me."

"Oh, baby." I let out a few moans, pushing my fingers in deeper. Then I feel the orgasm rising, just as Kenzie begins to whimper across the bed.

"Oh, Barbie!" she screams, and the toy goes flying out of her pussy and across the bed as she lets go and moans.

"Oh, fuck!" I call out, my own orgasm taking over as I watch how good she's fucked herself.

Both of us lie breathlessly on opposite sides of the bed. Our hair is splayed along the sheets, and our legs are shaking from our orgasms. She kisses the top of my head and begins playing with my hair.

"If that's how goodbye sex is going to go, I'm gonna have to say goodbye more often," Kenzie jokes.

"Oh, shush. Just you wait for the *I haven't seen you in weeks* sex. By then we should have a few new toys to play with," I say with a wink.

"Mmm, tell me more."

"Well, they'll probably be pink but they work just as well."

"You wouldn't be you if they were any other color." She laughs with me.

"I love you, Kenzie. Like my heart has never felt this full with another human before, and it's scary as hell but I hope you'll go easy with my heart. I may be named after a doll, but fuck, I'm not made of anything durable," I joke.

"I love you, too, Barbie. I promise to take care of your heart—and the rest of you. I never want to hurt you again. I swear we can make this work, and I will forever be grateful for this second chance, Doll Face," she adds, and I grimace at my nickname. Although, if she's the one calling me that, I might get used to it.

I lay with Kenzie and a tightness forms in my chest as I think about how she'll be spending the next few weeks in London, without me. That was what happened to us last time and we didn't survive it. I instantly start to panic but I guess it's written all over my face.

"Where did you just go Barbie?" Kenzie asks rubbing my cheek gently.

"I was thinking about London, what if the same things happen?"

Kenzie pauses, thinking about it for a moment. "Why don't you come visit with me?"

"W-what?"

"Not for a long time but even just a few days? Come see my life there, help me back up boxes and show you that I'm coming to New York whether you're ready for me or not." She laughs.

"I don't know about work..." I hesitate, then I think about all the sick days I've accumulated. "Actually, yes. I think that would make me feel a ton better." I smile.

"Then it's settled my love, you'll come visit and we can plan when I officially move to New York to make things easier on both of us." She smiles and kisses my cheek. I feel a thousand times better than I did a few minutes ago. But that's just how it was with Kenzie. She was someone who always made me feel better and loved.

Epilogue

Barbie

3 months later...

"Are you sure you can't just skip this shoot?" I ask Kenzie, even though I already know the answer. I don't want to go on this vacation without her, but I also don't want to come between her and her job.

"I'm sure. It wouldn't look good for me to be skipping shoots this early with a new agency." Kenzie sighs.

"I know, I know. I just wish you were coming with us." I huff.

"I know, but I'll be here when you get back to hear all about it." She smiles. I nod and lean forward to kiss her. It was meant to be a quick kiss but her tongue enters my mouth, and suddenly, I'm forgetting where we are.

HONK! HONK!

"COME ON, LOVE BIRDS!" Kelly calls from the car, and I pull back, rolling my eyes at my sister.

"Okay! I'm coming!" I say back.

"That's what she said." Kenzie winks and I hit her lightly on the shoulder.

"Don't encourage her with jokes please," I say, shaking my head.

"I love you!" She laughs.

"I love you, too." I kiss her one last time and then pick up my pink suitcase and put it in the back of the cab with Kelly's and hop in the back.

Kenzie's waving goodbye from the steps of our apartment—well, my apartment—that she moved into a few months ago. It was just easier than trying to find a brand-new place in this economy. Besides, I have my whole pink thing going on, and I don't want to change it. Thankfully, Kenzie's happy as long as she's living with me. The pink doesn't bother her, and her stuff from London fits in perfectly with mine. It's like we were made for each other.

"Mom and Dad are meeting us at the hotel. They took an earlier flight and don't wanna wait in the airport for us," Kelly says, looking up from her phone.

"Okay." I nod.

By the time we get to the hotel, I'm exhausted, and all I want is a glass of wine before I head to bed. Kelly and I drop our bags with the bellboy and head to the bar to meet our parents. They're both waiting with a glass of wine in front of them.

"How was your flight?" my mom asks with a smile.

"Rough," I grumble.

"We got seated apart for some reason, and there was a grumpy and very burly man between us," Kelly explains.

"Two glasses of Chardonnay, please," I tell the bartender. He nods and places two coasters in front of us.

"I'm sorry, loves." My mom frowns. "You should've flown first class like we did."

"I don't need to spend extra money on that, but I would like to sit next to my sister on the way home." I sigh. The bartender places the glass of wine in front of me, and I gulp down a few swigs.

"I'm sure you'll feel better in the morning." Kelly smiles.

"Yes, I plan to relax on the beach and soak in some sun. I think it's the first vacation I've been on in since our trip to London. I'm going to enjoy every second of it." Then I finish my wine and decide it's time for bed.

"You're going to bed?" my mom asks.

"Yes, I'm going to call Kenzie and say goodnight," I explain.

"Okay," they say in unison, each taking turns to hug me goodnight.

I head to the hotel room and decide to FaceTime Kenzie. Maybe we'll have FaceTime sex. Mmm, the idea alone just turns me on. But then I think about the time difference and realize she might be working or sleeping. I'm not in the mood to do the math, so when she doesn't pick up during my first try, I decide to text her and let her know I'm headed to bed. I'll have the whole week to coordinate talking to her.

IN THE MORNING, I head to the beach—alone—and find one of those lounge chairs claiming it as my own. I scroll on my phone and text Kenzie a few photos of the view. Maybe she'll see what she's missing out on and want to come next time. We haven't talked on the phone yet but she did text me to say good morning and that she hopes I'm having a good time.

I soak in the sun and relax in the kid-free spot of the hotel. There's no chance of running into anyone under eighteen, and I can relax easily.

I'm supposed to meet my parents for dinner but besides that, I have nothing planned for the day. So I lie around on the beach, drink the day away, and swim in the sparkling, blue ocean. It's even more beautiful than the California oceans I'm used to.

About halfway through the day, Kelly joins me on the beach. We order more cocktails and then head for the pool.

"Are you bummed Kenzie couldn't join us?" she asks after a quick dip. She's reading on her Kindle while I'm scrolling through my phone.

"Yeah, but I'm hoping she'll be able to make the next trip." It isn't like we never go on vacation.

"That's true, it'll be weird with you bringing someone, though. Next time I'll have to bring a friend or something," she says with a shrug.

"Why not bring someone you're seeing? Get back out there or something," I tease, repeating the words she said to me before Kenzie came back into my life.

"Oh, hush. I'm in my single era, and I plan to soak up every moment of it," she says, and I roll my eyes, sliding my pink heart shades down over my eyes. It's what I had planned to do, too—well, kind of. I was focusing solely on my career until my girl stumbled back into my life, and the rest is history.

"Whatever you say," I add with a shrug.

"So how's everything with the board?" Kelly asks and I smile.

"Perfect, no longer an issue." One of the board members dropped out, causing an open seat which meant we needed to hire someone new. What they didn't expect was to find someone who was such a fan of the way I ran things that she refused to vote their way. So as long as she has a job, my job is safe.

"Ah, that's a relief." Kelly beams.

We head to dinner with Mom and Dad after changing into our dressy clothes for the night. Kelly insisted we dress up for the night even though I'm exhausted and just wanted to throw on a pair of shorts and a T-shirt. She even did my makeup for me and curled my hair. I can't remember the last time the two of us were so dressed up for dinner, let alone a dinner with our parents.

"You girls look nice." My dad smiles and greets us both with a kiss.

"I don't know why we couldn't just come here from the beach, but Kelly insisted," I say with a shrug. She's the baby of the family and usually gets everything she wants.

"Well, you look beautiful." My mom grins and takes a sip of her drink.

We enjoy a quiet dinner at the Seaside Café, which has a wonderful view of the beach. I bet this spot is incredibly beautiful at sunset, but for some reason my parents wanted to have dinner earlier than usual. It's barely five o'clock, and we're almost finished eating already. I'll definitely be taking advantage of room service later tonight.

"Want to join us for a walk on the beach?" my parents ask. I'm surprised. I know I don't go on a ton of vacations with them anymore, but we usually just meet up for meals and do our own thing the rest of the time.

"I don't know," I say.

"Come on! It'll be fun!" Kelly adds.

"You're going?" Part of me will feel bad if I bail.

"I am." She smiles as if we're going on some big trip and not just a walk on the beach.

"Alright, well, if you're all going, I guess I will," I say with a shrug. I planned on watching the sunset on the beach tonight anyway.

We make our way to the beach, Kelly and I taking off our heels to walk in the sand. Our parents walk hand in hand in front of us. We're following their lead but I'm about to stop them from walking when I spot someone standing near a big sign that reads: *Marry Me*. It's written in big block letters, all lit up, and I don't want my oblivious parents to get in the way of someone's proposal.

"Wait ..." I trail off as I look at the woman in the black dress. *Is that ... Kenzie ...?*

"Go!" Kelly pushes me slightly as a huge grin spreads on her face, and I almost fall headfirst into the sand. *Wouldn't that be a sight?*

My parents and Kelly stick behind me as I walk closer and closer to Kenzie. She's standing in the sand behind a pink runway she's clearly created. It looks like it's made out of fabric, and it leads a trail straight to where she's standing. Pink rose petals are dispersed everywhere I look and light pink candles are flickering in the wind. A bottle of what I assume to be champagne rests in the sand. My eyes skim over the bottle and then take in my surroundings again. I gasp as my heart beats out of control. She's pulled out all the stops.

"Barbie, I hope you're okay with this surprise." She beams as I get close enough.

"I'm shocked, honestly," I tell her, feeling like I'm living in a dream. "What happened to your shoot?" I ask, suddenly concerned about her new job. I hope she didn't put off work because of me again.

"I didn't actually have one. It was just a lie to get me

here to surprise you," she explains. I step closer to her, and she smiles, taking my hands in hers.

"I love you, Barbara Ann, and I will continue loving you as long as our days allow. I lost you once, and I never plan on doing that again. I can't imagine my life without you, and I hope you feel the same. We are Barbie and Ken-zie. Built for each other for life. Will you do me the incredible honor of being my wife?" Kenzie gets down on one knee, and my hands go to my mouth in shock. Even though I saw this coming once I spotted her, those words are unexpected.

"I would love to! Yes!" I squeal, jumping up and pulling her in for a kiss. She dips me, our lips lingering as my parents and Kelly howl in excitement—along with the small crowd of people that's accumulated.

She pops open the box with the ring and shows me a light pink, oval-shaped diamond ring with a silver band. It's exquisite. Breathtaking. Entirely me and exactly what I want on my hand until the end of time. I beam, Kenzie takes the ring from the box and places it on my ring finger.

"I love you." I smile, gazing at the ring and then back at Kenzie.

"I love you, too." We kiss again, this time longer and more intimately.

"These are for you." She pulls away and hands me a bouquet of pink roses. Then she bends down to grab the bottle of champagne, pops it, and my family runs over with empty flutes.

"Congratulations!" my mom and dad say in unison. My sister takes my hand and gushes at the ring. There's what seems like a bunch of never-ending hugs from everyone.

I can't believe I'm engaged to the woman I love. It seems as if she pulled it off effortlessly, too. She holds me as we look at the beautiful pink and orange sunset in front of us.

She orchestrated this entire ordeal to happen at the perfect moment; the waves crash against the shore, and the sun is swallowed by the horizon. It's something I'll try to remember for the rest of our lives.

"Barbie, I love you," Kenzie says, holding my hand and gazing at the ring.

"Don't you worry, had I known you were planning this I would've brought yours," I say with a wink.

"What?" She looks at me with wide eyes.

"Your proposal is coming baby, just you wait." I smile. "I can't have my model fiancée walking around without a ring, now can I?" I ask with a smirk.

"I guess you can't." She laughs.

I know exactly how I'm going to ask her. I just have to sneak her away to the place where we first met without her realizing.

Acknowledgments

Thank you to Lily of Lily Bear Designs Co. for making this pre-made that sparked this story idea. I love your creativity and how you can always whip up something sapphic for me.

Thank you to my auntie Christine for always playing with Barbies with me when I was little. This is a very grown up version of playing with Barbies that you definitely shouldn't read.

Thank you to my ARC team and all the ARC readers of this book. Especially to Laci for Beta/Alpha reading for me when I decided writing a book a week was a good idea.

Thanks to Michelle for keeping me on track and convincing me to write this book. I thought I couldn't do it but she kicked my butt into gear. Without her we might not have gotten this book, especially not in a week.

Thanks to my sprinting buddies S.E. Green & JJ Grice, ya'll are the best and keep me on track better than I ever could.

Thanks to all of you who picked up this book and gave my writing a chance. It truly means the world to me.

Also by Shannon O'Connor

SEASONS OF SEASIDE SERIES

(each book can be read as a standalone)

Only for the Summer

Only for Convenience

Only for the Holidays

SWEET IN SEASIDE

(Each book can be read as a standalone)

Sweet on You

Sweet as Honey

Sprinkled with Love

Semisweet for You

ETERNAL PORT VALLEY SERIES

Unexpected Departure

Unexpected Days

STANDALONES

Electric Love

Butterflies in Paris

All's Fair in Love & Vegas

Fumbling into You

Doll Face

THE HOLIDAYS WITH YOU

(each book can be read as a standalone)

I Saw Mommy Kissing the Nanny

Lucky to be Yours

The Only Reason

Ugly Sweater Christmas

POETRY

For Always

Holding on to Nothing

Say it Everyday

Midnights in a Mustang

Five More Minutes

When Lust Was Enough

Isolation

All of Me

Lost Moments

Cosmic

About the Author

Shannon O'Connor is a twenty-something, bisexual, self-published poet of several books and counting. She released her first novel, *Electric Love* in 2021 and is currently working on a sapphic romance novel set for summer 2022. She is often found in coffee shops, probably writing about someone she shouldn't be.

Heat. Heart. & HEA's.

Check out more work & updates on:
Facebook Group: https://www.facebook.com/groups/shanssquad

Website: https://shanoconnor.com

Printed in Great Britain
by Amazon